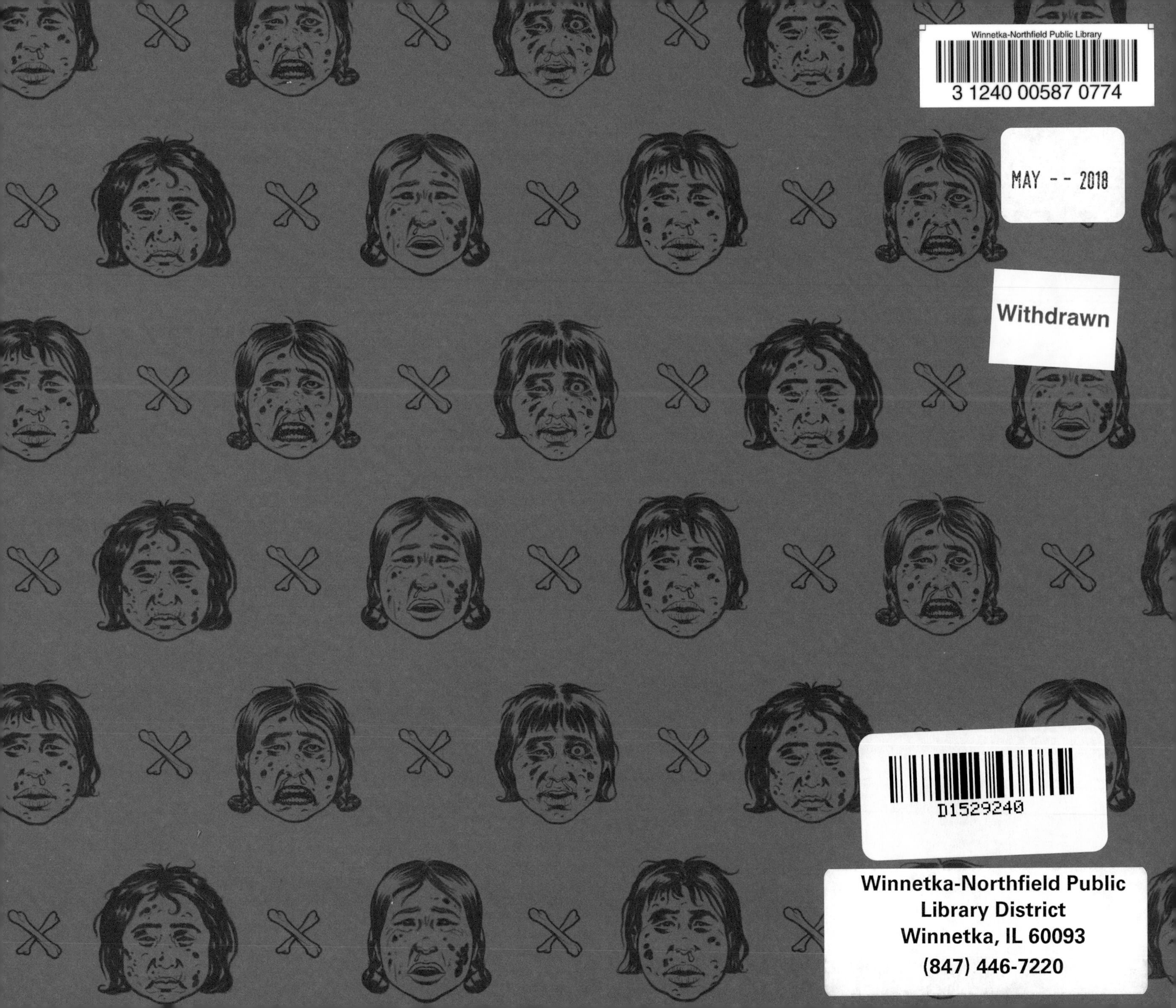

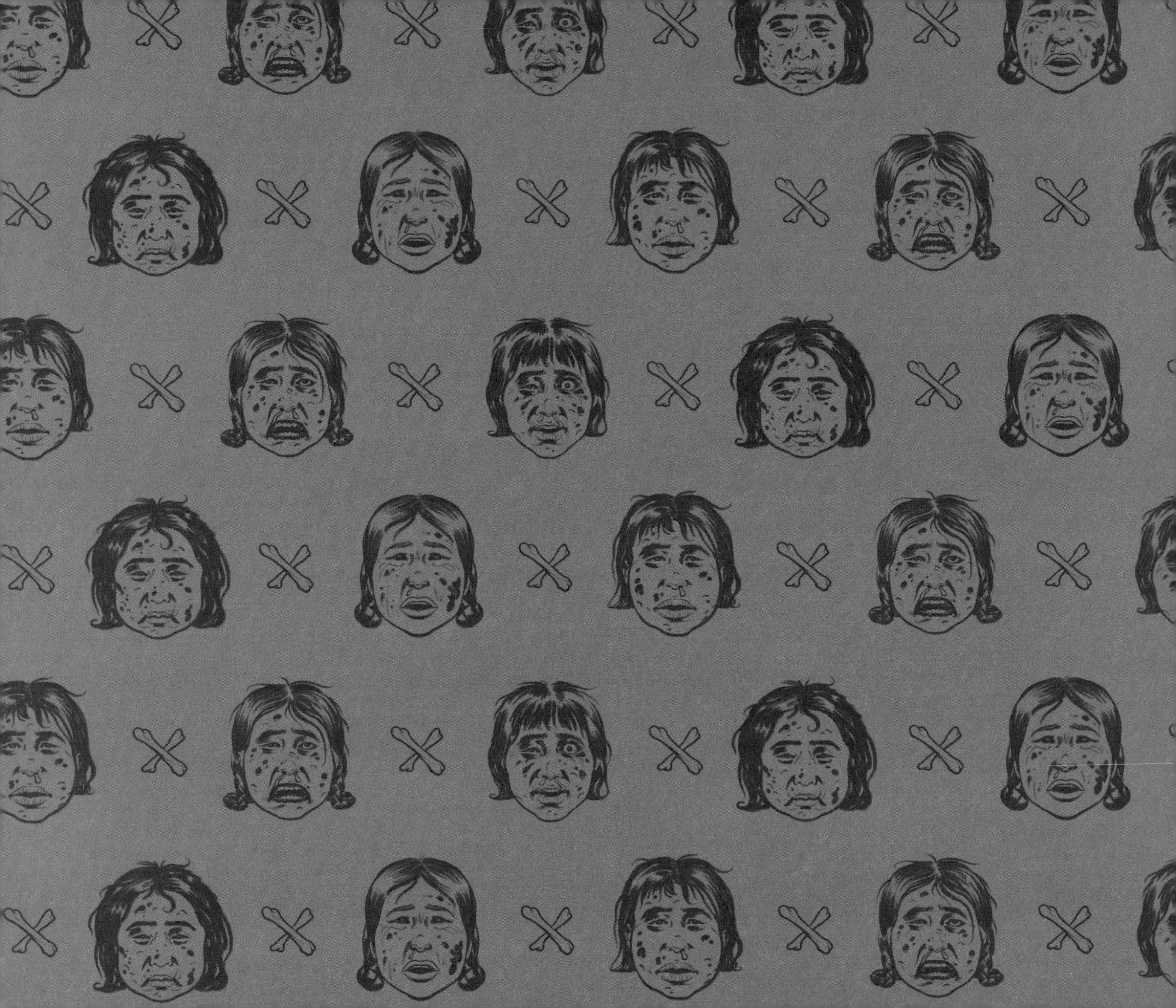

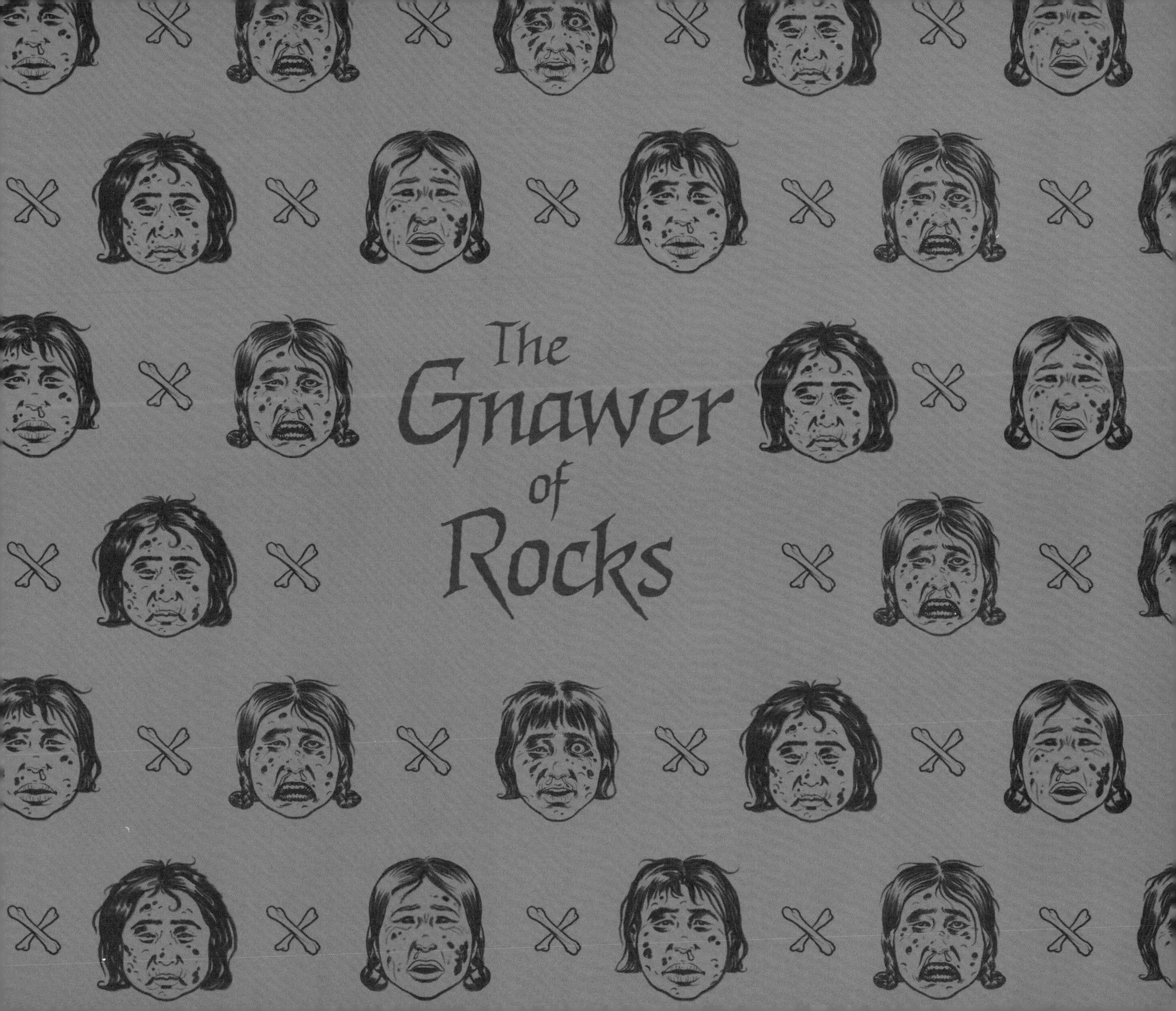
The
Gnawer
of
Rocks

PUBLISHED BY INHABIT MEDIA INC.
WWW.INHABITMEDIA.COM

INHABIT MEDIA INC. (IQALUIT) P.O. BOX 11125, IQALUIT, NUNAVUT, XOA 1HO
(TORONTO) 191 EGLINTON AVE. EAST, SUITE 301, TORONTO, ONTARIO, M4P 1K1

DESIGN AND LAYOUT COPYRIGHT © 2017 BY INHABIT MEDIA INC.
TEXT COPYRIGHT © 2017 BY LOUISE FLAHERTY
ILLUSTRATIONS BY JIM NELSON COPYRIGHT © 2017 INHABIT MEDIA INC.

STORY ADAPTED TO GRAPHIC NOVEL BY NEIL CHRISTOPHER
EDITED BY NEIL CHRISTOPHER AND DANIELLE WEBSTER
ART DIRECTION BY NEIL CHRISTOPHER
DESIGN BY ASTRID ARIJANTO

WE ACKNOWLEDGE THE SUPPORT OF THE CANADA COUNCIL FOR THE ARTS FOR OUR PUBLISHING PROGRAM.

THIS PROJECT HAS BEEN MADE POSSIBLE IN PART BY THE GOVERNMENT OF CANADA.

ISBN: 978-1-77227-165-2

LIBRARY AND ARCHIVES CANADA CATALOGUING IN PUBLICATION

FLAHERTY, LOUISE, AUTHOR
THE GNAWER OF ROCKS / BY LOUISE FLAHERTY ; ILLUSTRATED
BY JIM NELSON.

ISBN 978-1-77227-165-2 (HARDCOVER)

1. GRAPHIC NOVELS. I. NELSON, JIM, 1962–, ILLUSTRATOR
II. TITLE.

PN6733.F55G63 2017   j741.5'971   C2017-904588-1

PRINTED IN CANADA.

The Gnawer of Rocks

BY **LOUISE FLAHERTY** · ILLUSTRATED BY **JIM NELSON**

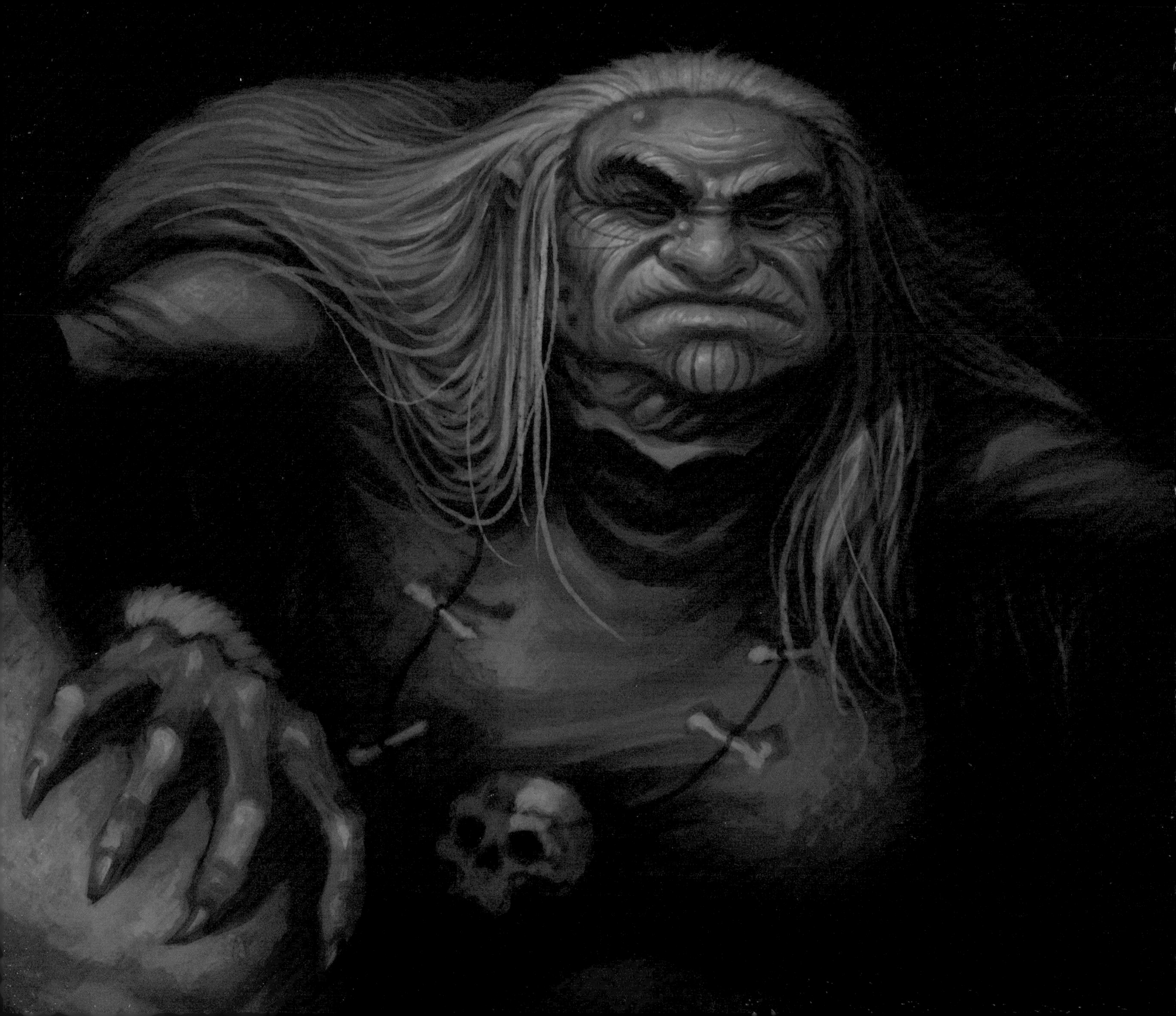

AUTHOR'S NOTE

THIS LEGEND IS PROBABLY QUITE DISTURBING TO SOMEONE WHO HAS NOT BEEN EXPOSED TO THE KIND OF GORY DETAILS OFTEN FOUND IN INUIT STORIES.

I FIRST HEARD THIS TRADITIONAL TALE FROM AN INUK STORYTELLER, LEVI IQALUGJUAQ, WHO WOULD COME TO OUR PORTABLE CLASSROOM FROM TIME TO TIME IN CLYDE RIVER IN THE 1970S TO SHARE STORIES THAT HE HAD HEARD FROM HIS FAMILY.

ONCE IQALUGJUAQ ARRIVED, WE WOULD GATHER AROUND HIM IN A SEMICIRCLE WITHOUT HIM EVER ASKING US TO SIT AROUND HIM. WE JUST DID. WHEN HE STARTED TELLING STORIES, WE WOULD BE SO ENGROSSED IN THE WAY HE TOLD THE STORY——HE HAD SUCH A CAPTIVATING TONE. IT WAS AS IF WE WERE WATCHING A TELEVISION SHOW.

THE FOLLOWING PAGES ARE HOW I REMEMBER THIS STORY . . .

—LOUISE FLAHERTY, IQALUIT

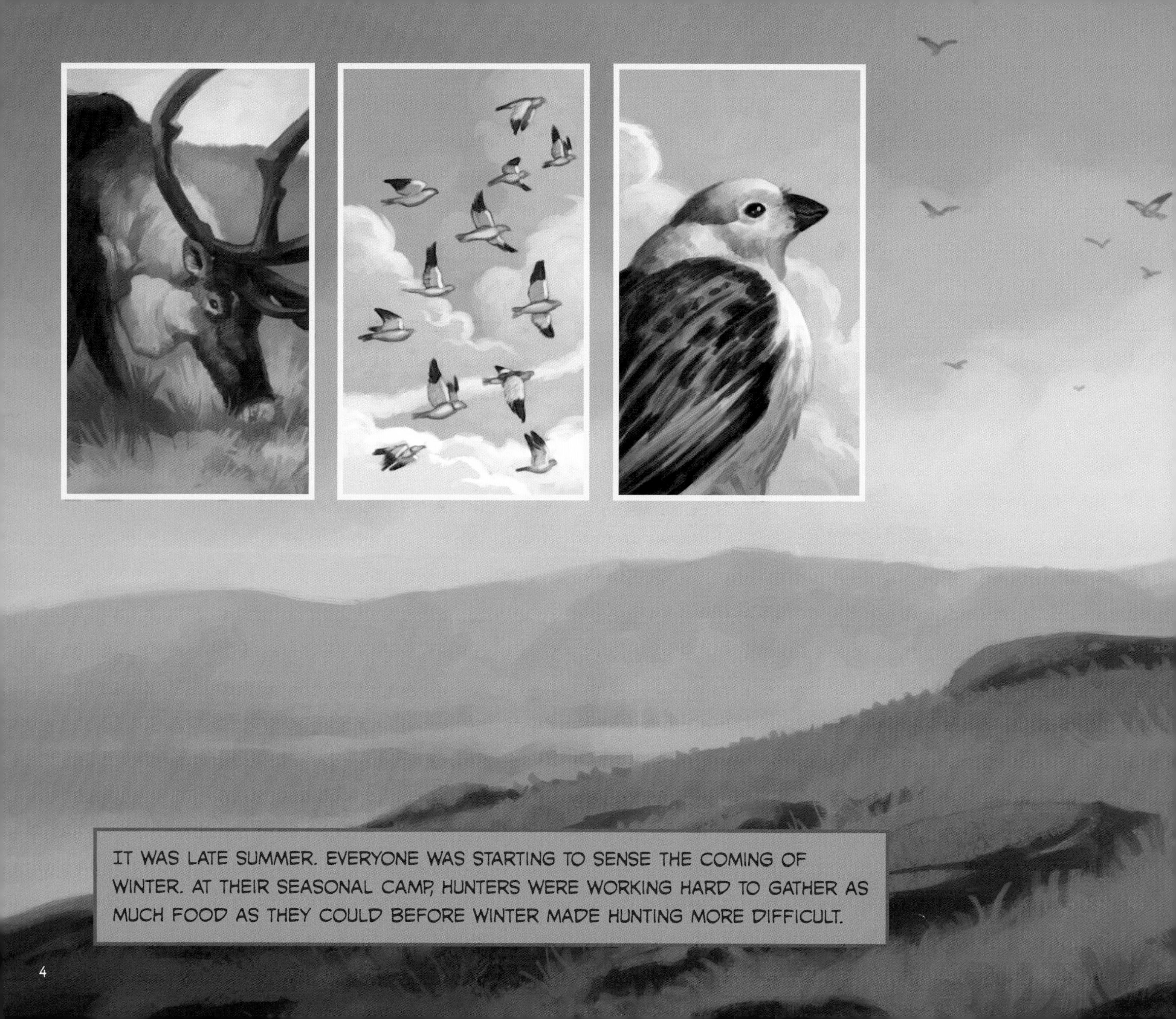
IT WAS LATE SUMMER. EVERYONE WAS STARTING TO SENSE THE COMING OF WINTER. AT THEIR SEASONAL CAMP, HUNTERS WERE WORKING HARD TO GATHER AS MUCH FOOD AS THEY COULD BEFORE WINTER MADE HUNTING MORE DIFFICULT.

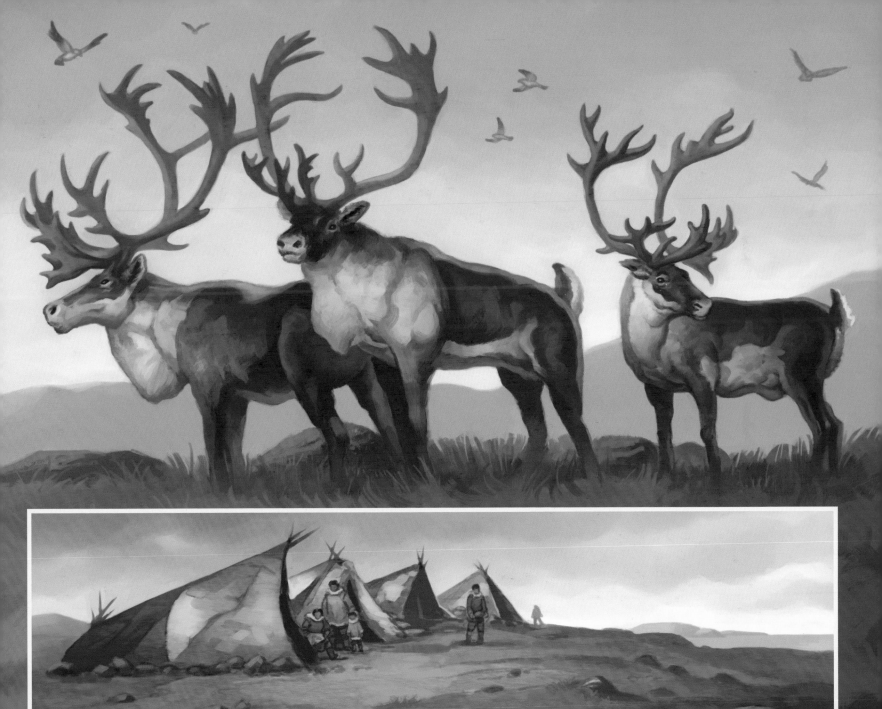

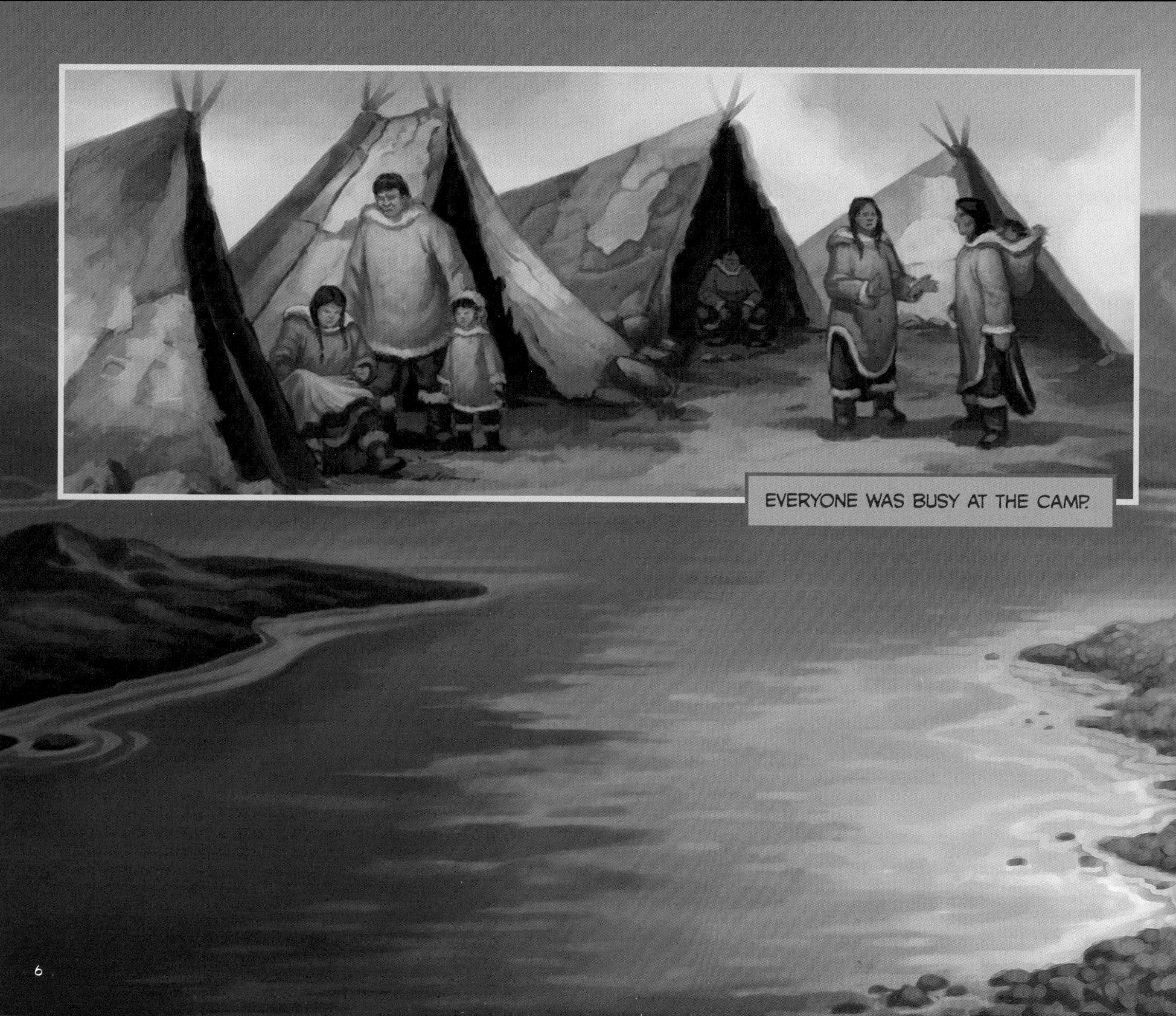
EVERYONE WAS BUSY AT THE CAMP.

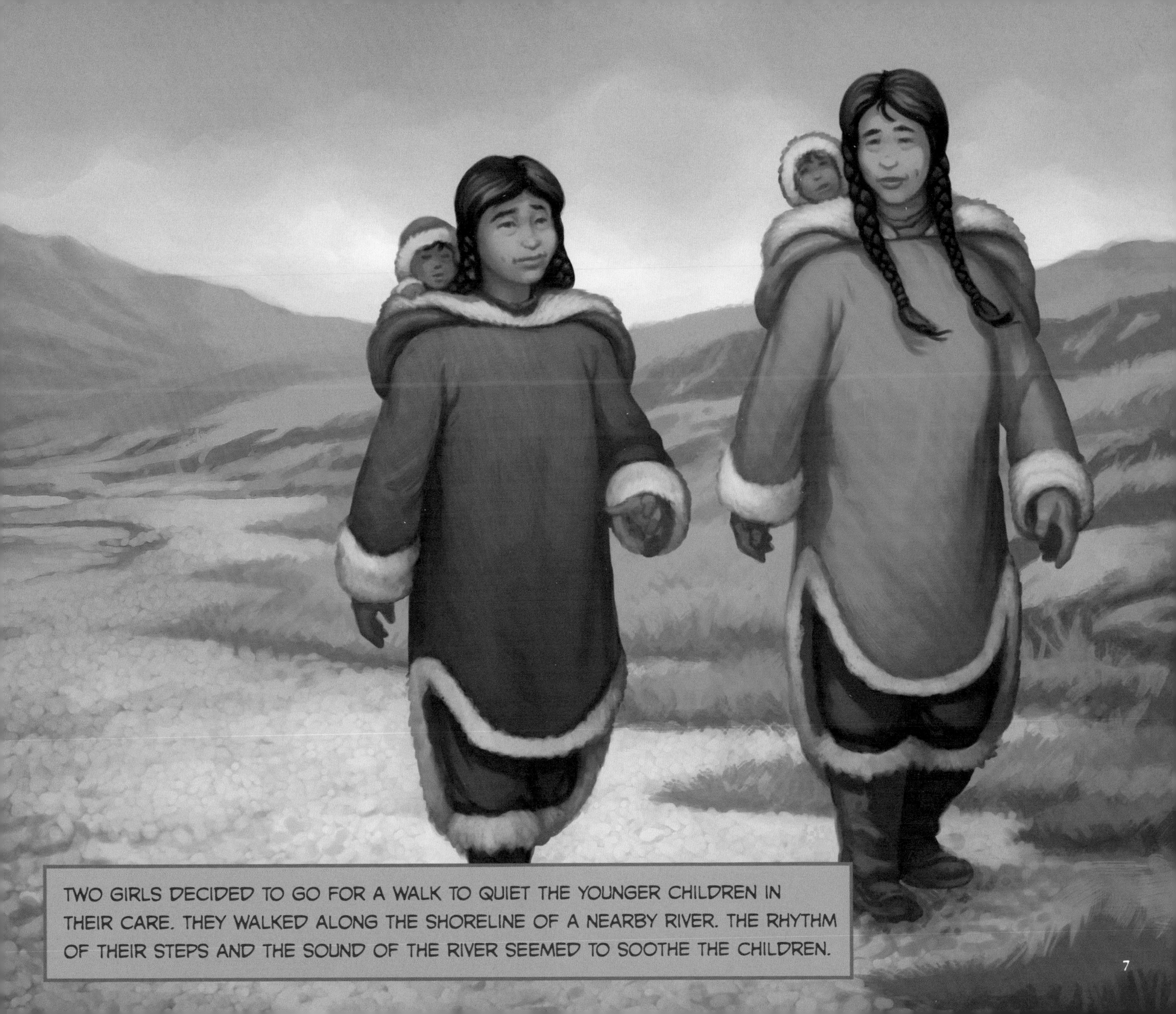

TWO GIRLS DECIDED TO GO FOR A WALK TO QUIET THE YOUNGER CHILDREN IN THEIR CARE. THEY WALKED ALONG THE SHORELINE OF A NEARBY RIVER. THE RHYTHM OF THEIR STEPS AND THE SOUND OF THE RIVER SEEMED TO SOOTHE THE CHILDREN.

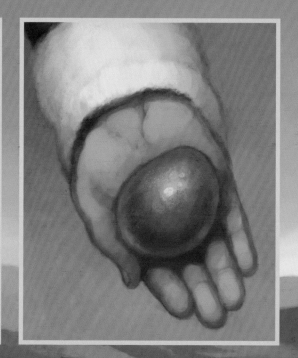

AS THEY WERE WALKING, ONE OF THE GIRLS FOUND AN UNUSUALLY SMOOTH AND SHINY STONE. THEY FOUND MORE STONES LIKE IT ALONG THE RIVER, ONE AFTER ANOTHER. EACH STONE WAS LOVELIER THAN THE ONE BEFORE. THE GIRLS WERE SO EXCITED THAT THEY DID NOT WATCH WHERE THEY WERE GOING.

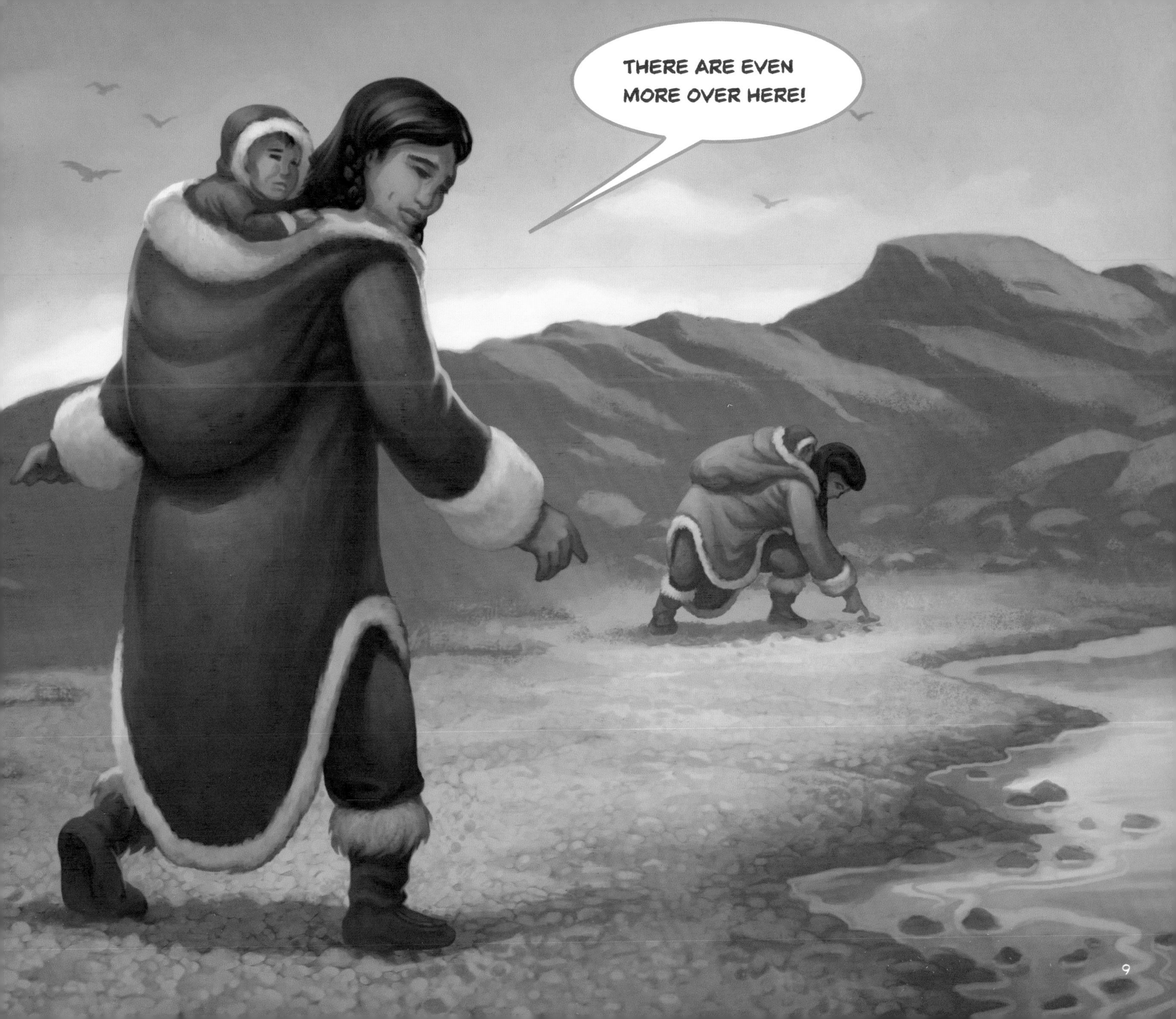
THERE ARE EVEN MORE OVER HERE!

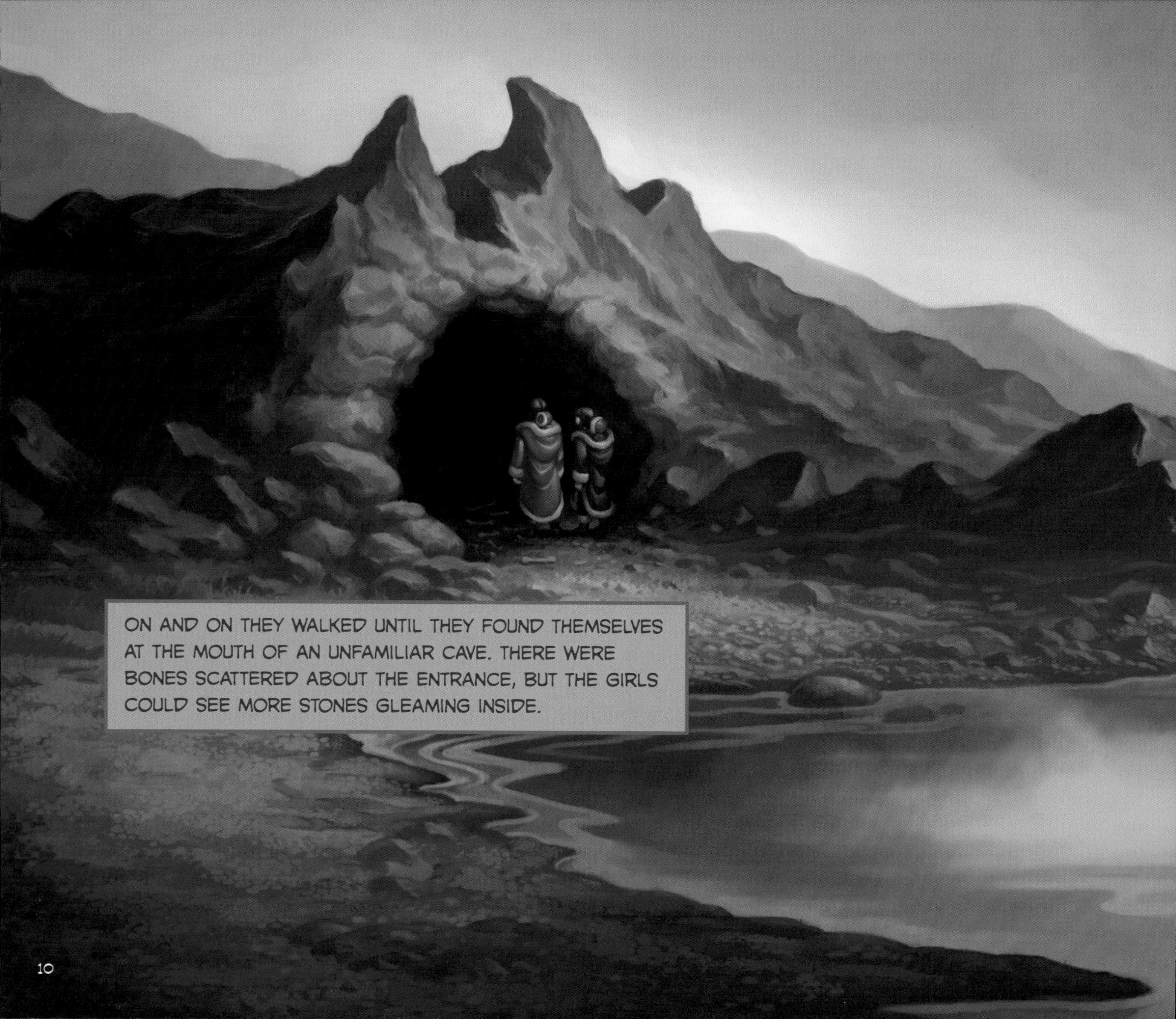
ON AND ON THEY WALKED UNTIL THEY FOUND THEMSELVES AT THE MOUTH OF AN UNFAMILIAR CAVE. THERE WERE BONES SCATTERED ABOUT THE ENTRANCE, BUT THE GIRLS COULD SEE MORE STONES GLEAMING INSIDE.

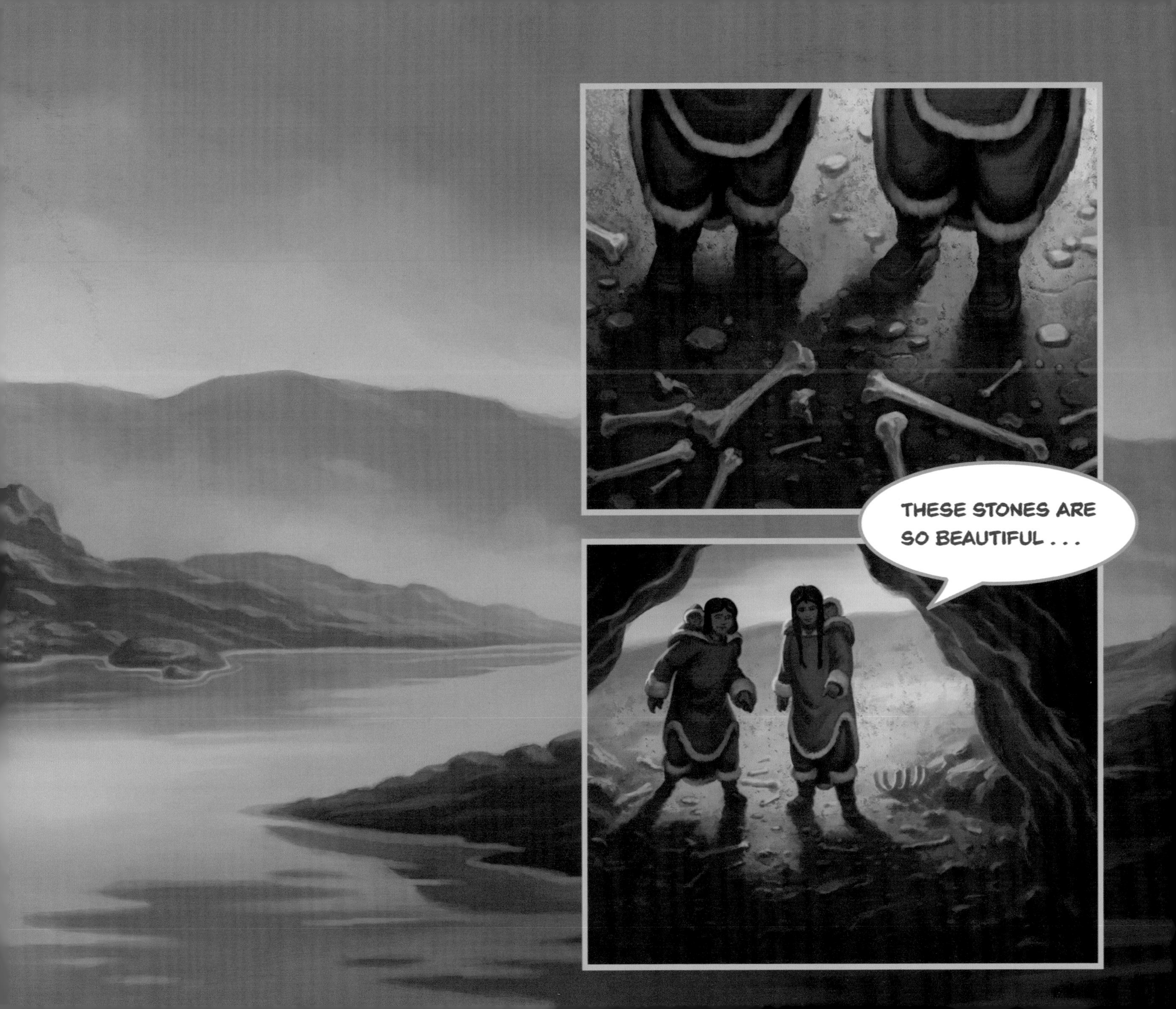
THESE STONES ARE SO BEAUTIFUL . . .

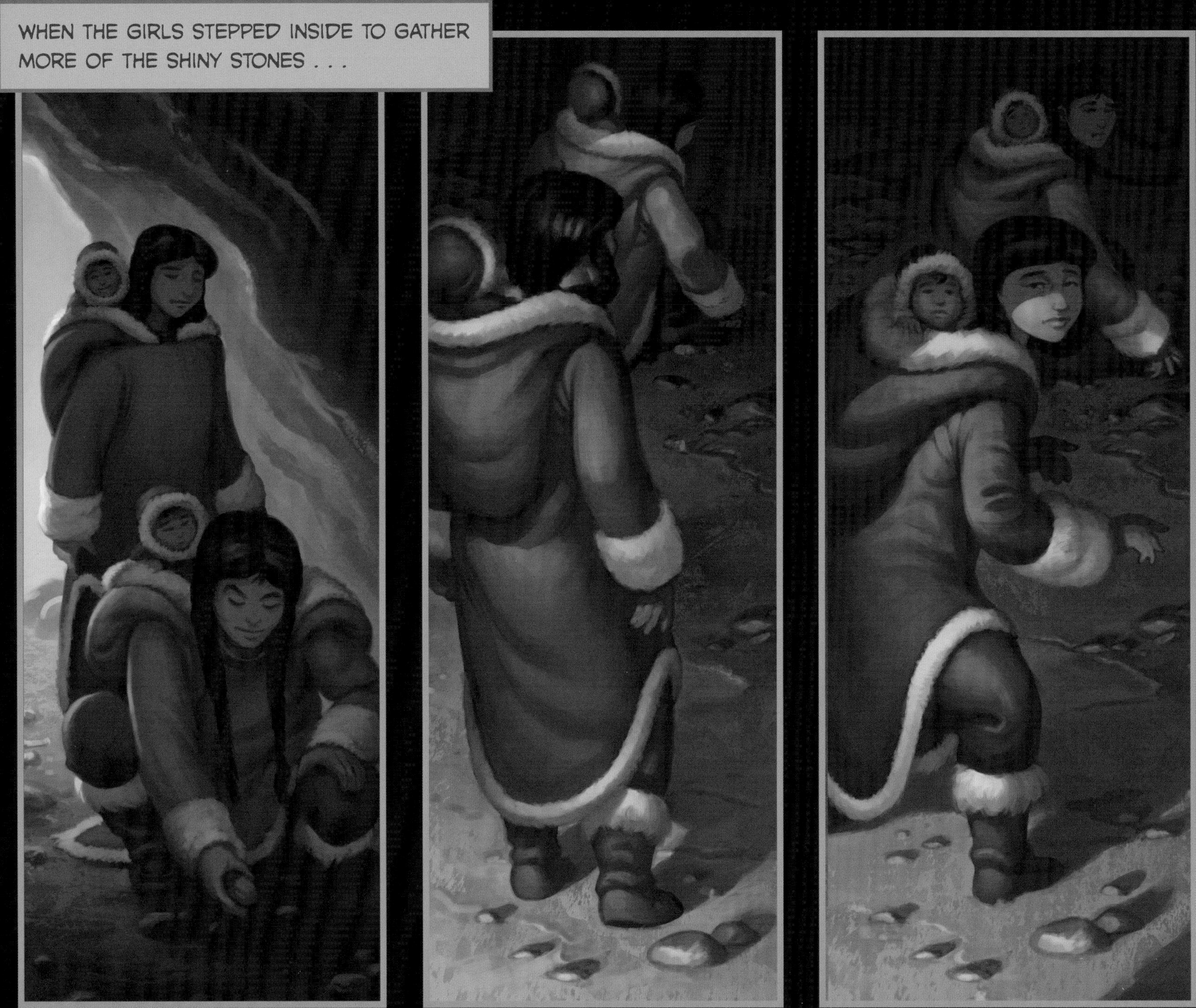
WHEN THE GIRLS STEPPED INSIDE TO GATHER MORE OF THE SHINY STONES . . .

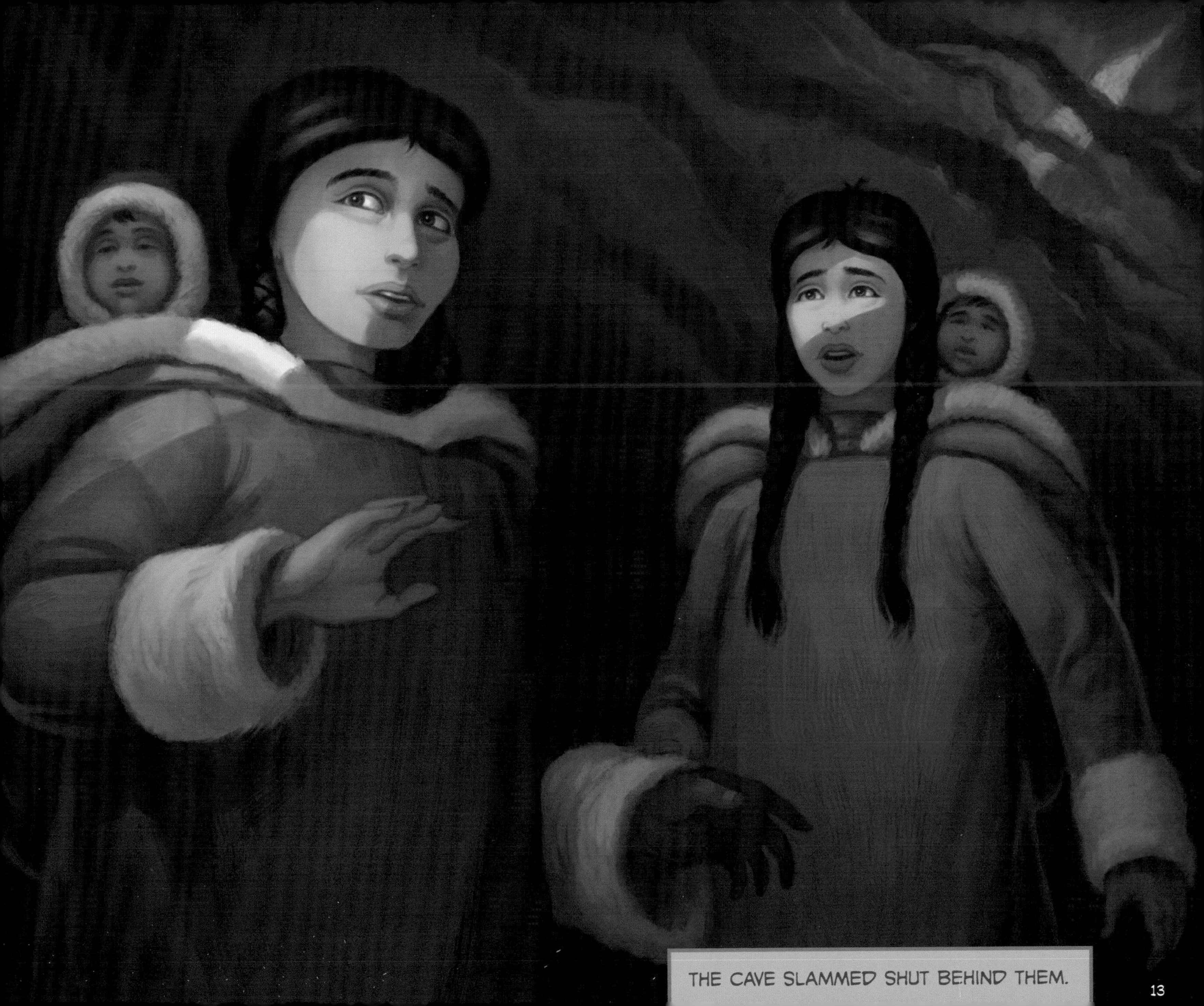
THE CAVE SLAMMED SHUT BEHIND THEM.

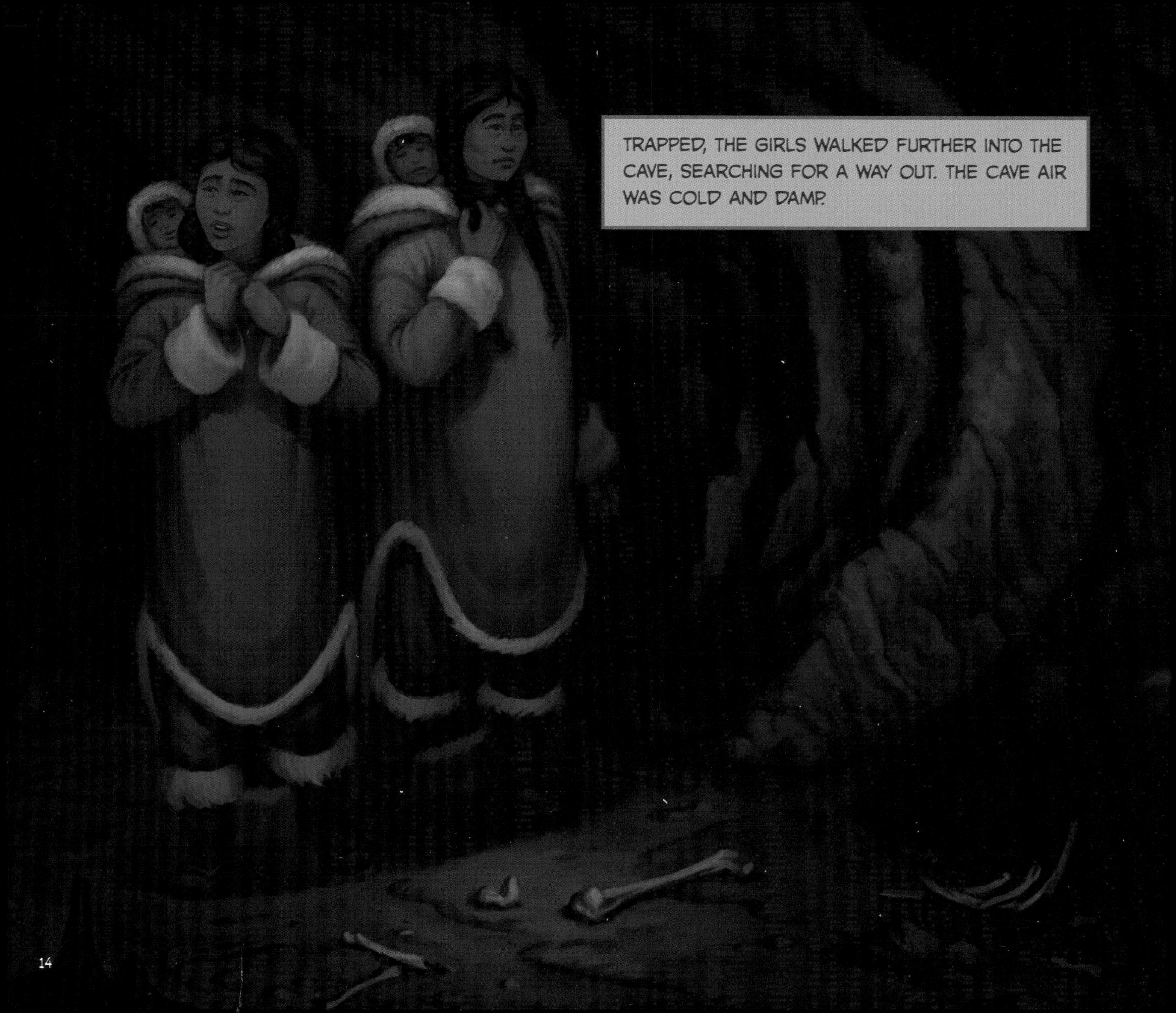
TRAPPED, THE GIRLS WALKED FURTHER INTO THE CAVE, SEARCHING FOR A WAY OUT. THE CAVE AIR WAS COLD AND DAMP.

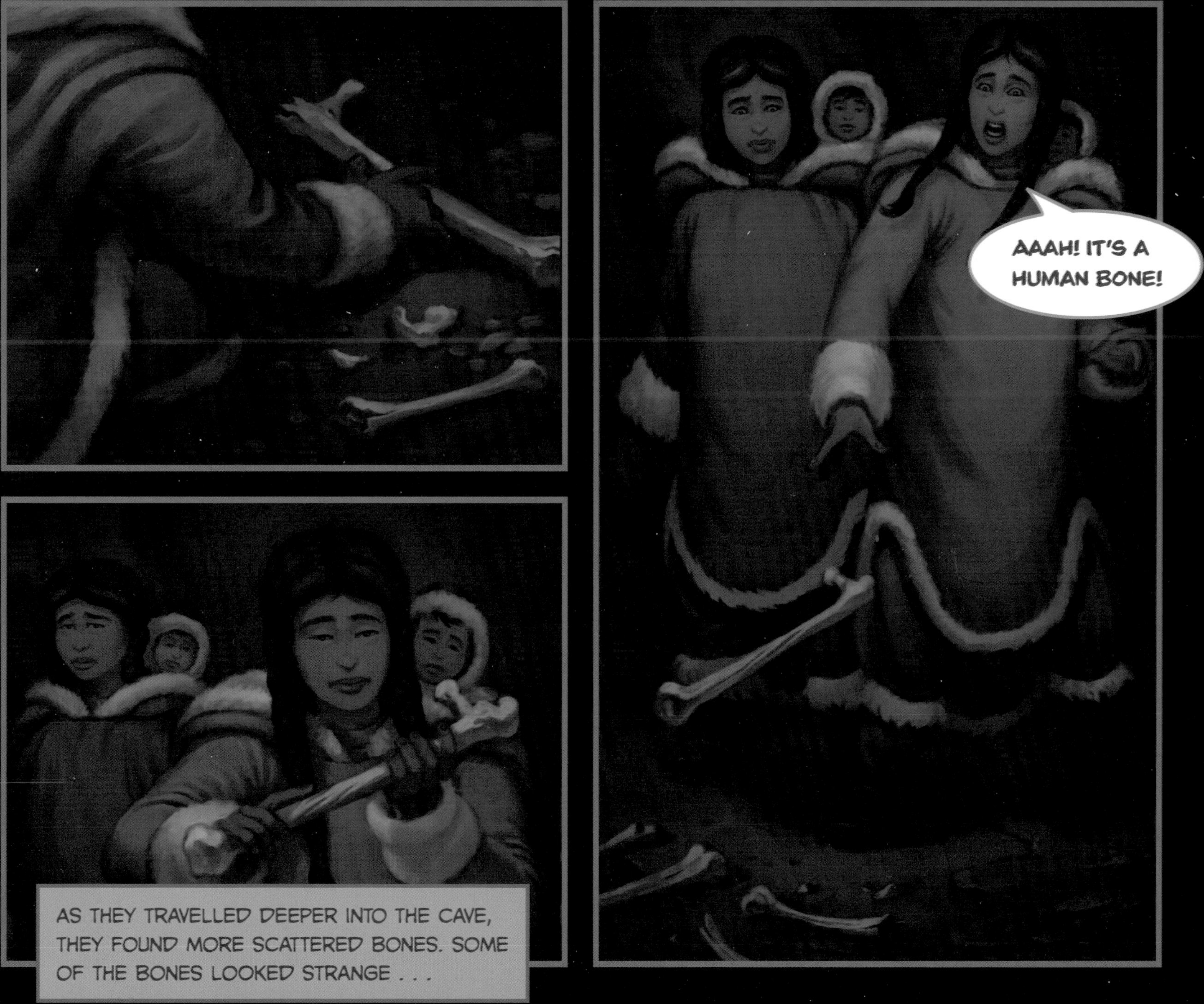
AS THEY TRAVELLED DEEPER INTO THE CAVE, THEY FOUND MORE SCATTERED BONES. SOME OF THE BONES LOOKED STRANGE . . .
AAAH! IT'S A HUMAN BONE!

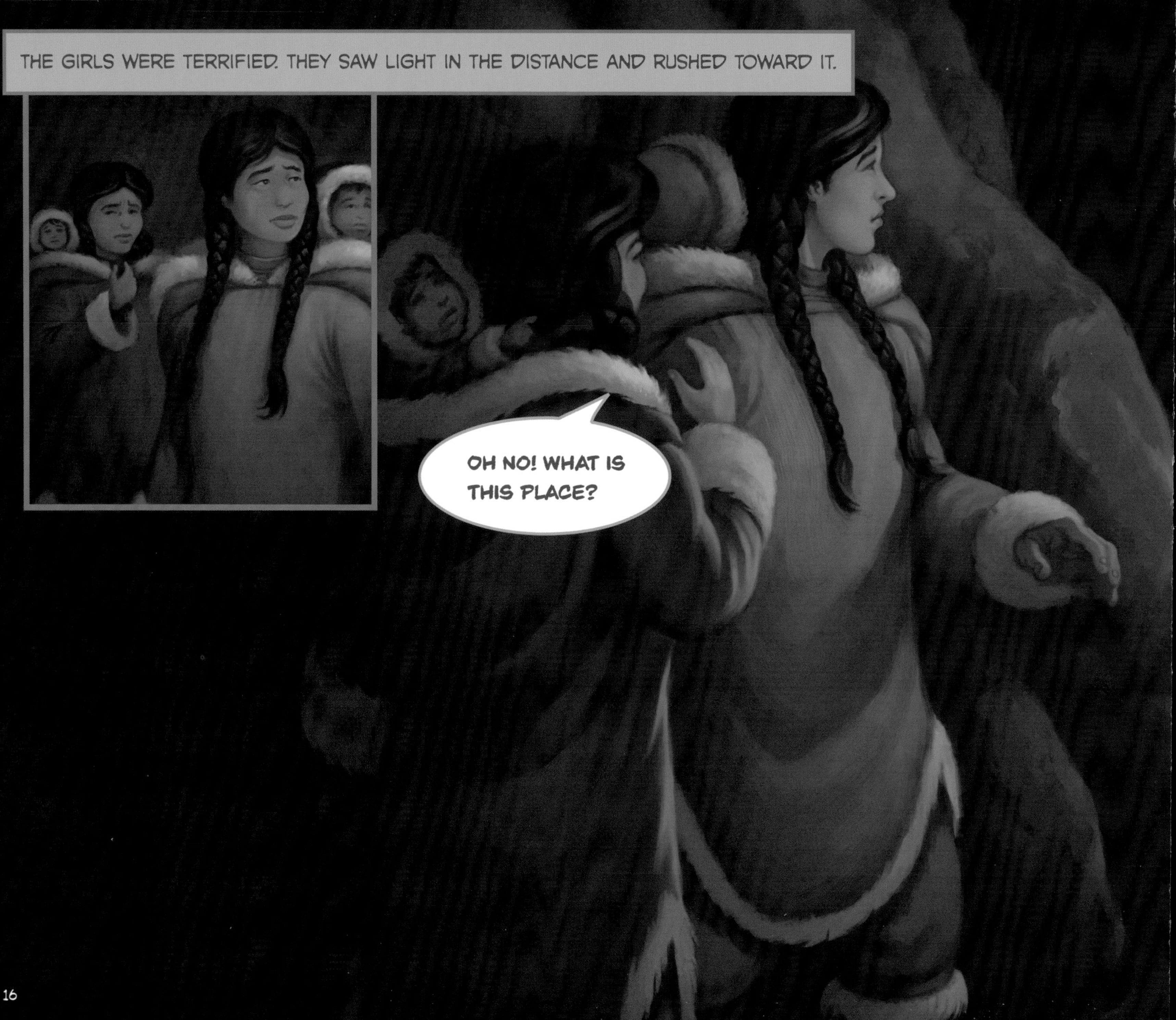
THE GIRLS WERE TERRIFIED. THEY SAW LIGHT IN THE DISTANCE AND RUSHED TOWARD IT.
OH NO! WHAT IS THIS PLACE?

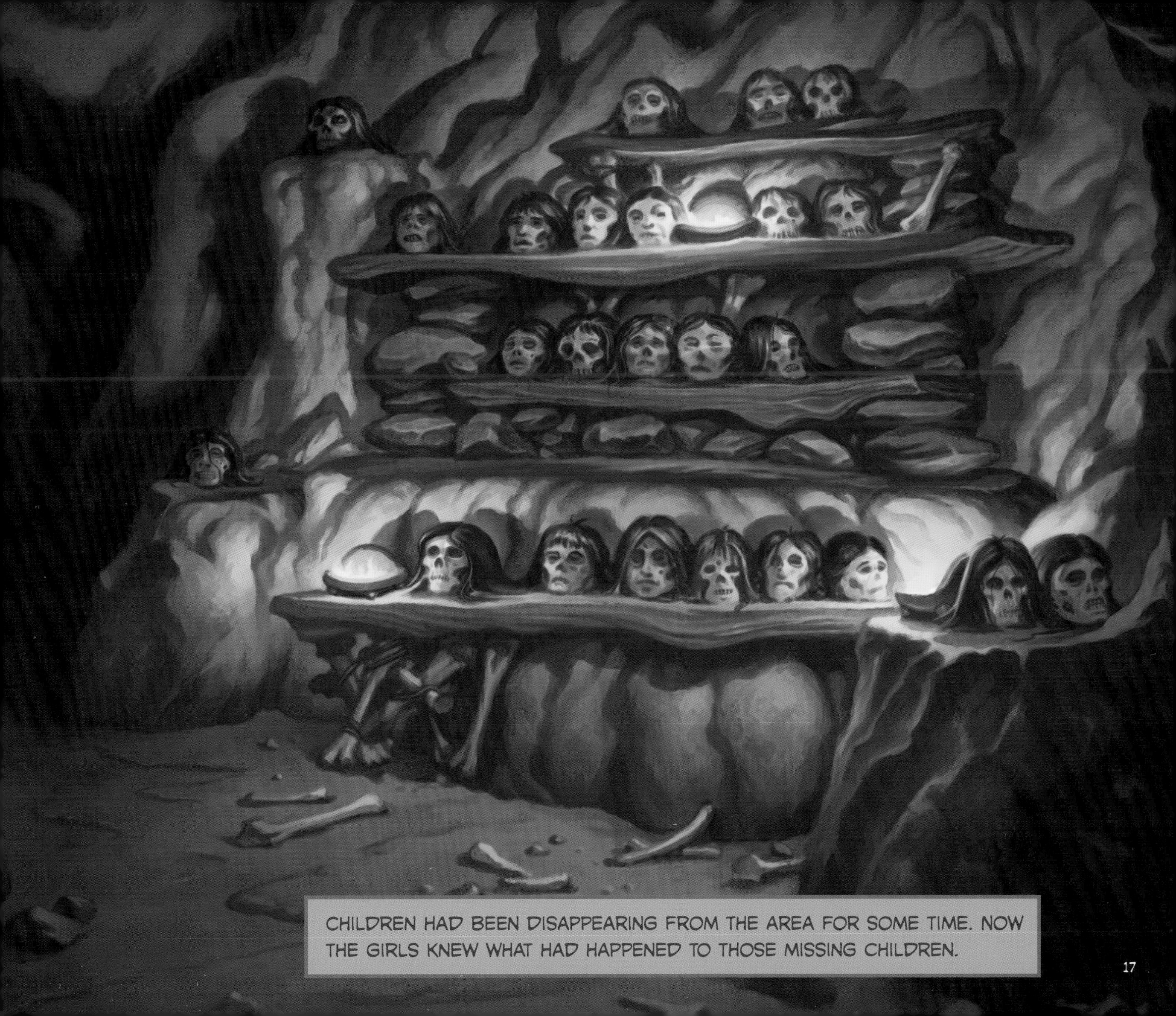
CHILDREN HAD BEEN DISAPPEARING FROM THE AREA FOR SOME TIME. NOW THE GIRLS KNEW WHAT HAD HAPPENED TO THOSE MISSING CHILDREN.

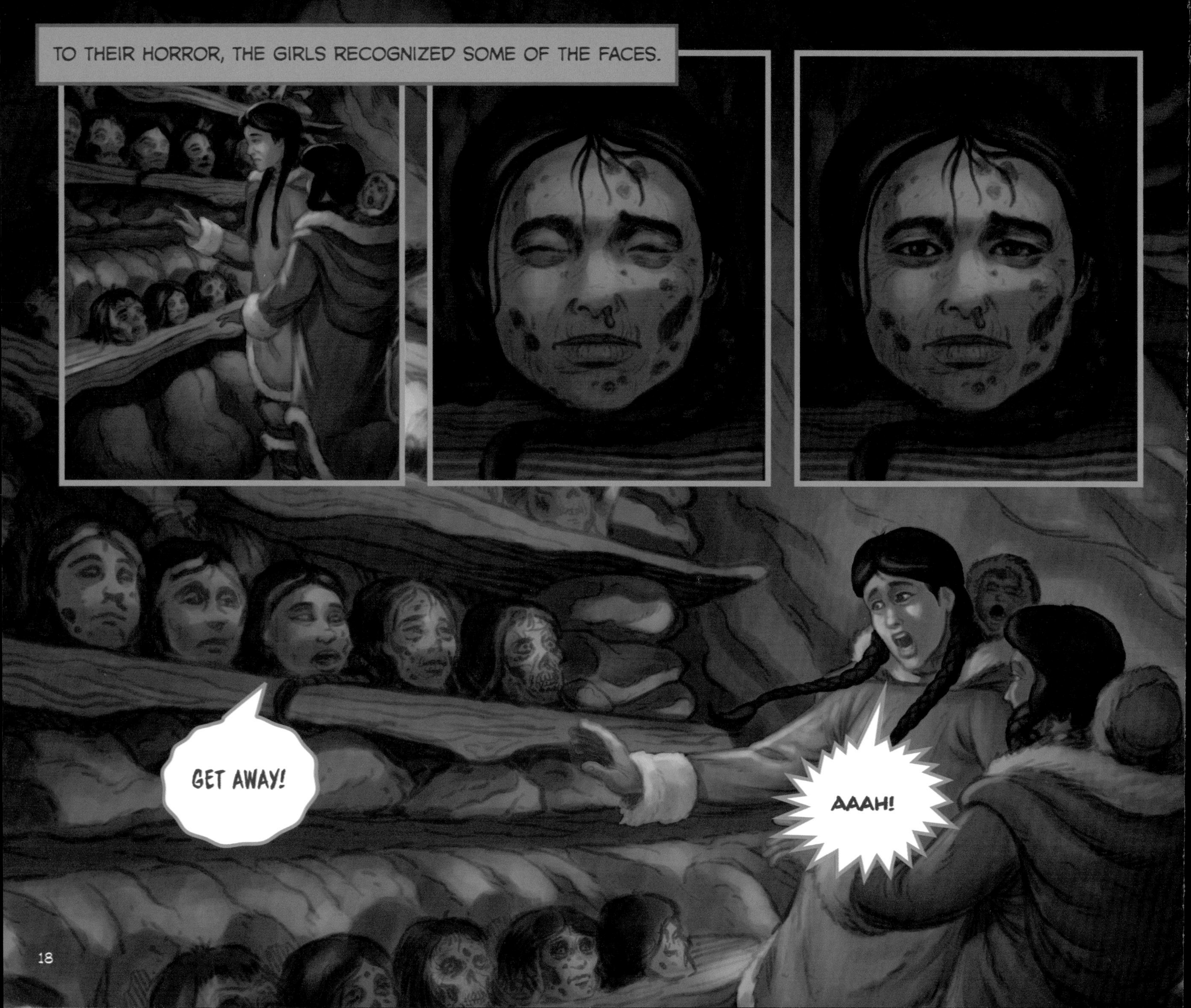
TO THEIR HORROR, THE GIRLS RECOGNIZED SOME OF THE FACES.
GET AWAY!
AAAH!

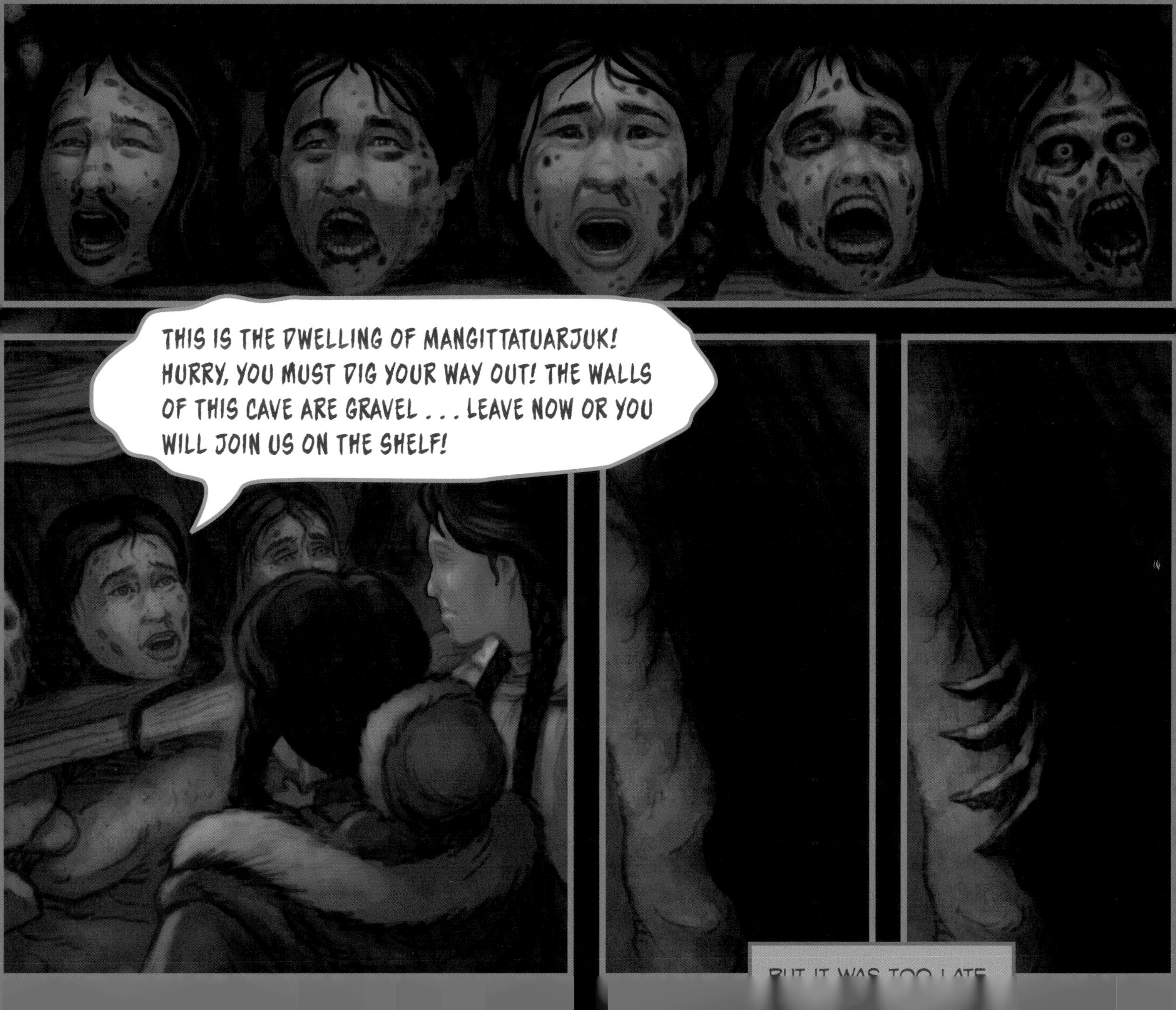
THIS IS THE DWELLING OF MANGITTATUARJUK! HURRY, YOU MUST DIG YOUR WAY OUT! THE WALLS OF THIS CAVE ARE GRAVEL . . . LEAVE NOW OR YOU WILL JOIN US ON THE SHELF!

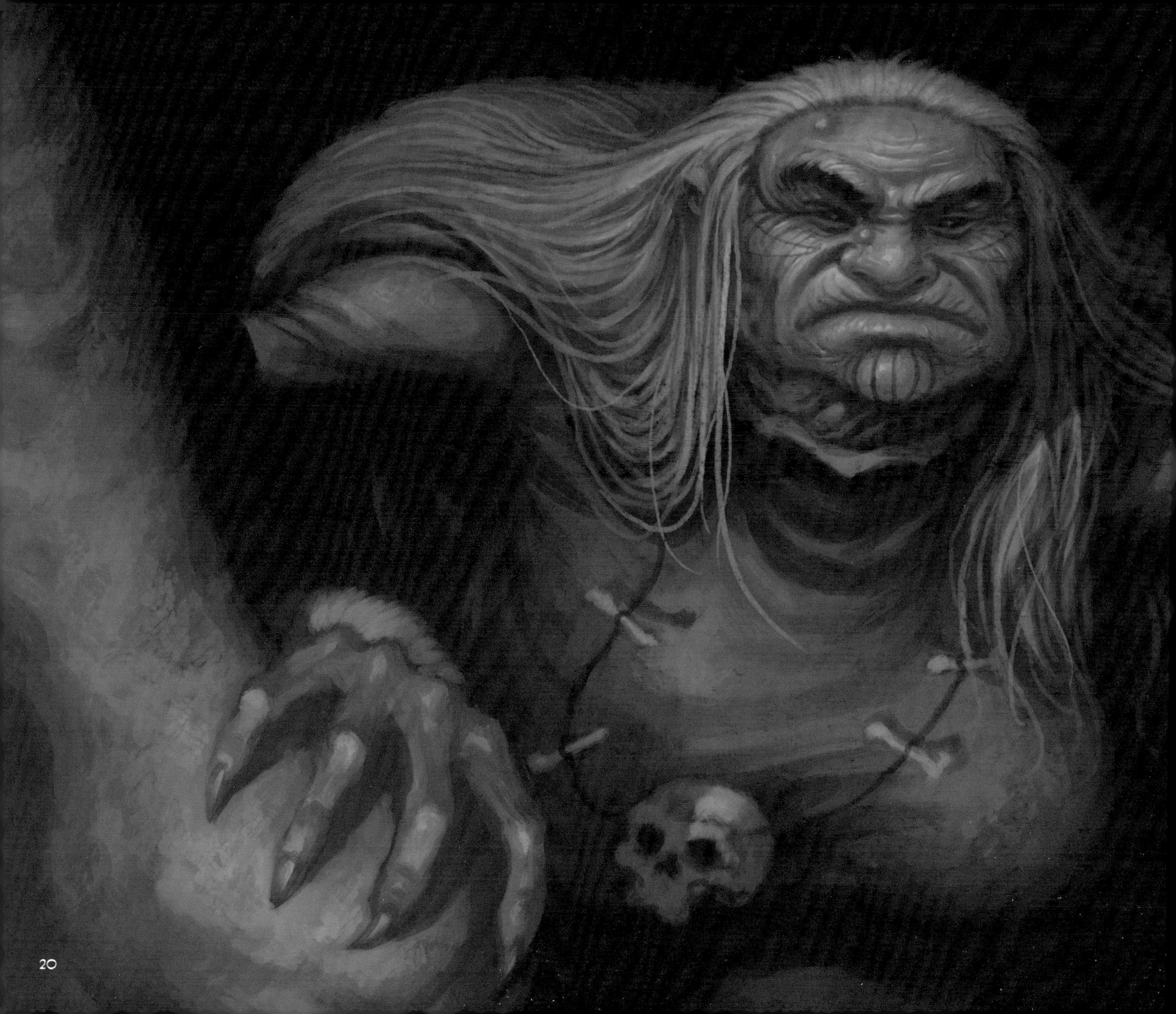

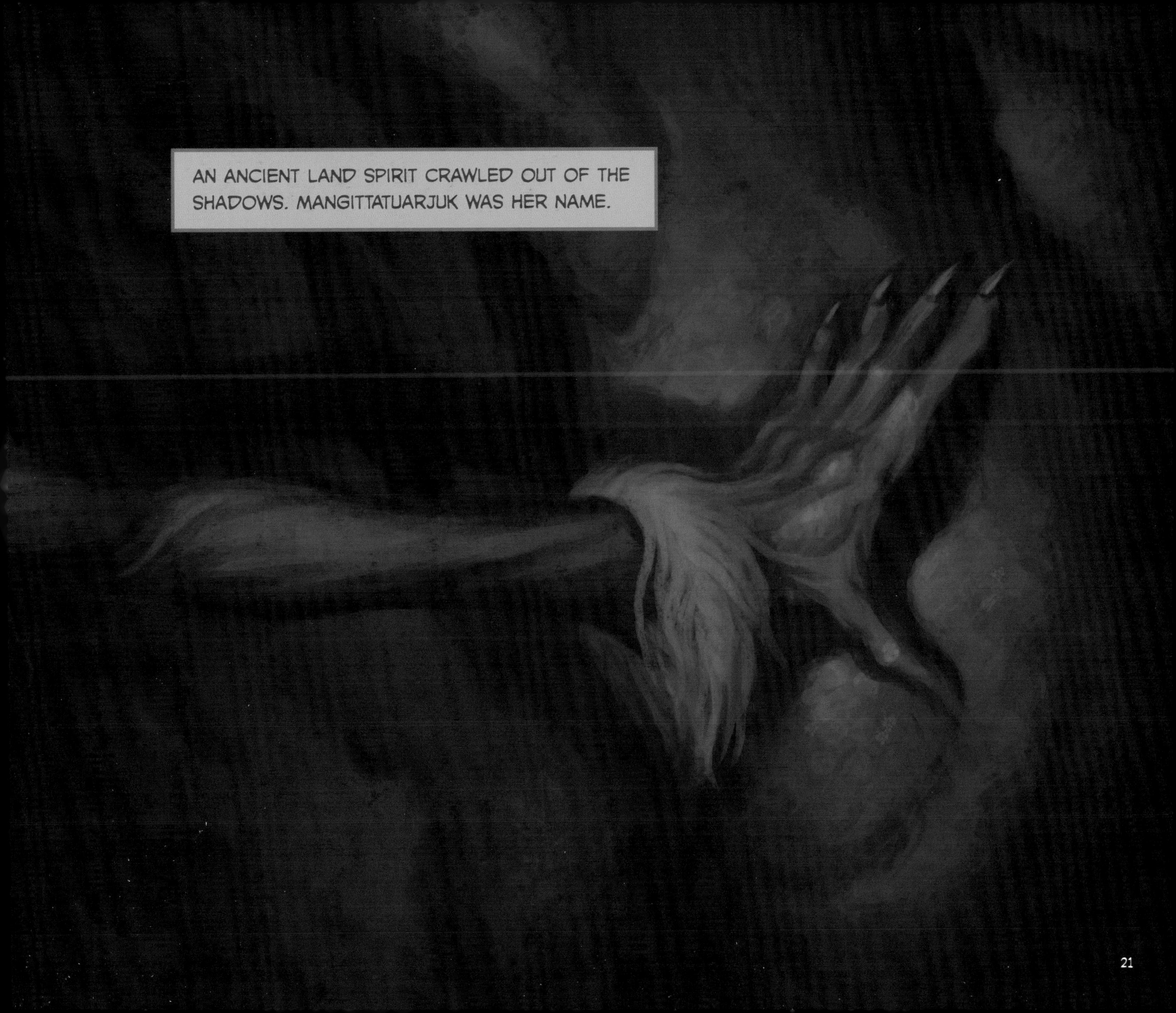
AN ANCIENT LAND SPIRIT CRAWLED OUT OF THE SHADOWS. MANGITTATUARJUK WAS HER NAME.

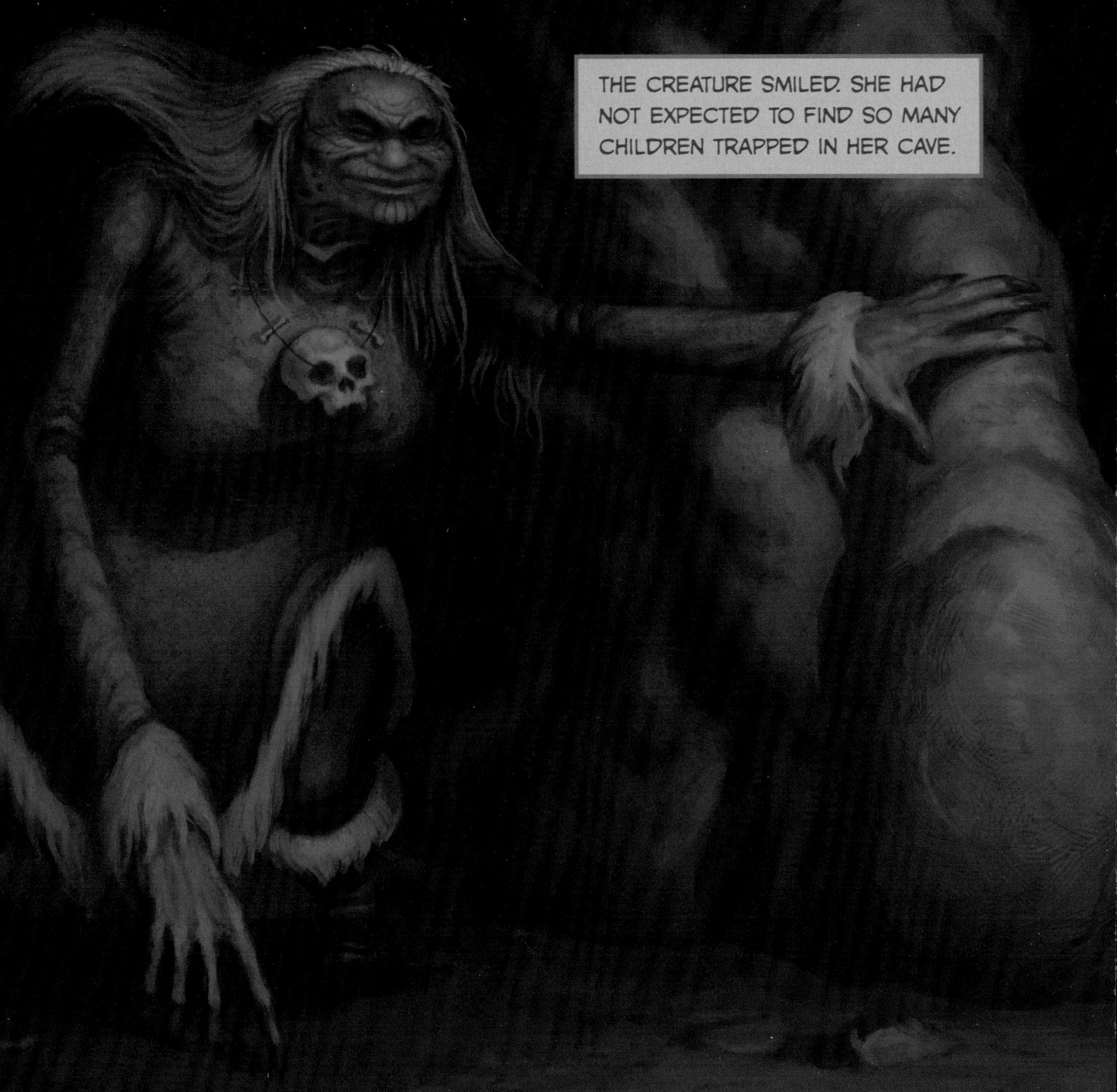
THE CREATURE SMILED. SHE HAD NOT EXPECTED TO FIND SO MANY CHILDREN TRAPPED IN HER CAVE.

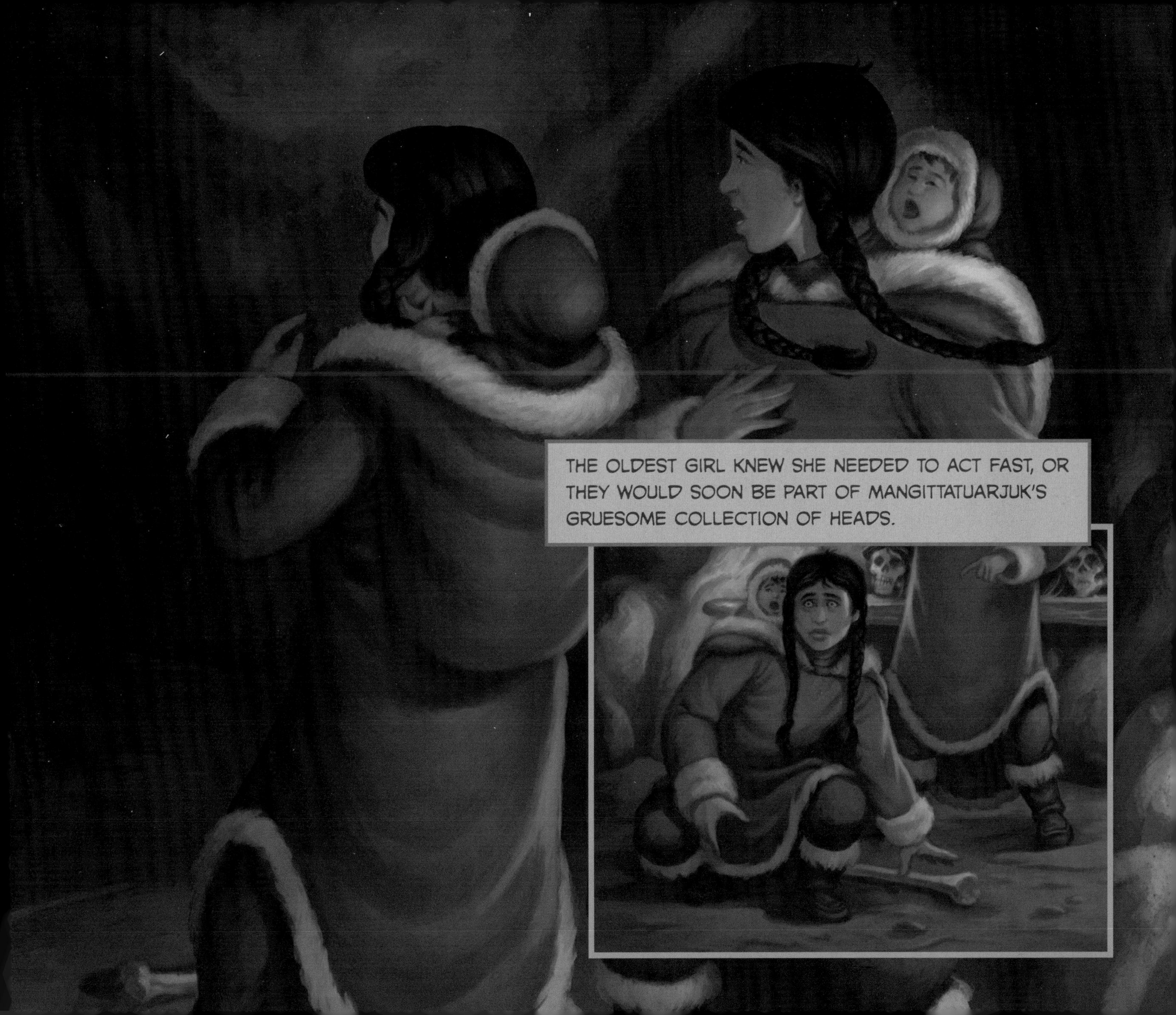
THE OLDEST GIRL KNEW SHE NEEDED TO ACT FAST, OR THEY WOULD SOON BE PART OF MANGITTATUARJUK'S GRUESOME COLLECTION OF HEADS.

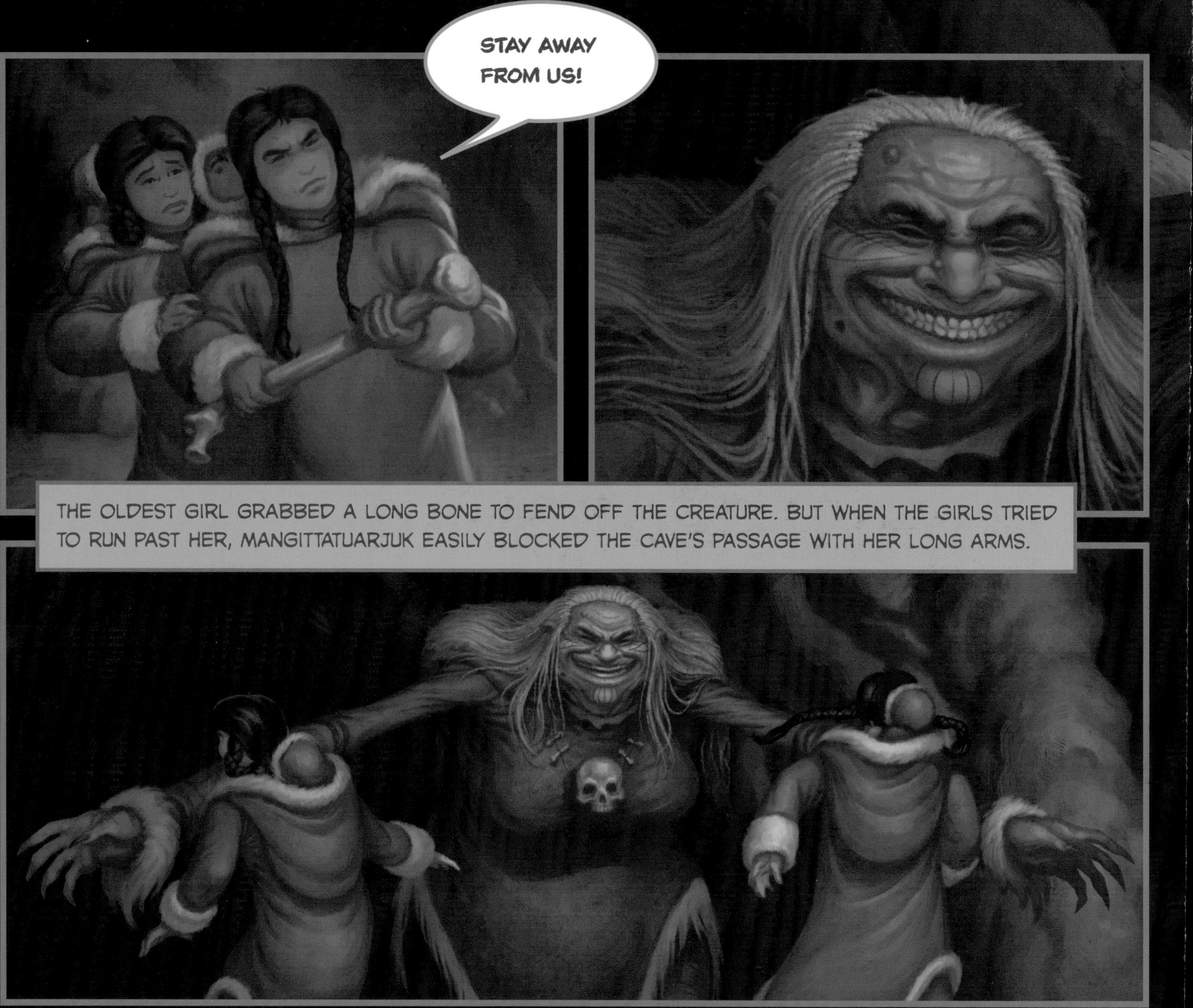
STAY AWAY FROM US!
THE OLDEST GIRL GRABBED A LONG BONE TO FEND OFF THE CREATURE. BUT WHEN THE GIRLS TRIED TO RUN PAST HER, MANGITTATUARJUK EASILY BLOCKED THE CAVE'S PASSAGE WITH HER LONG ARMS.

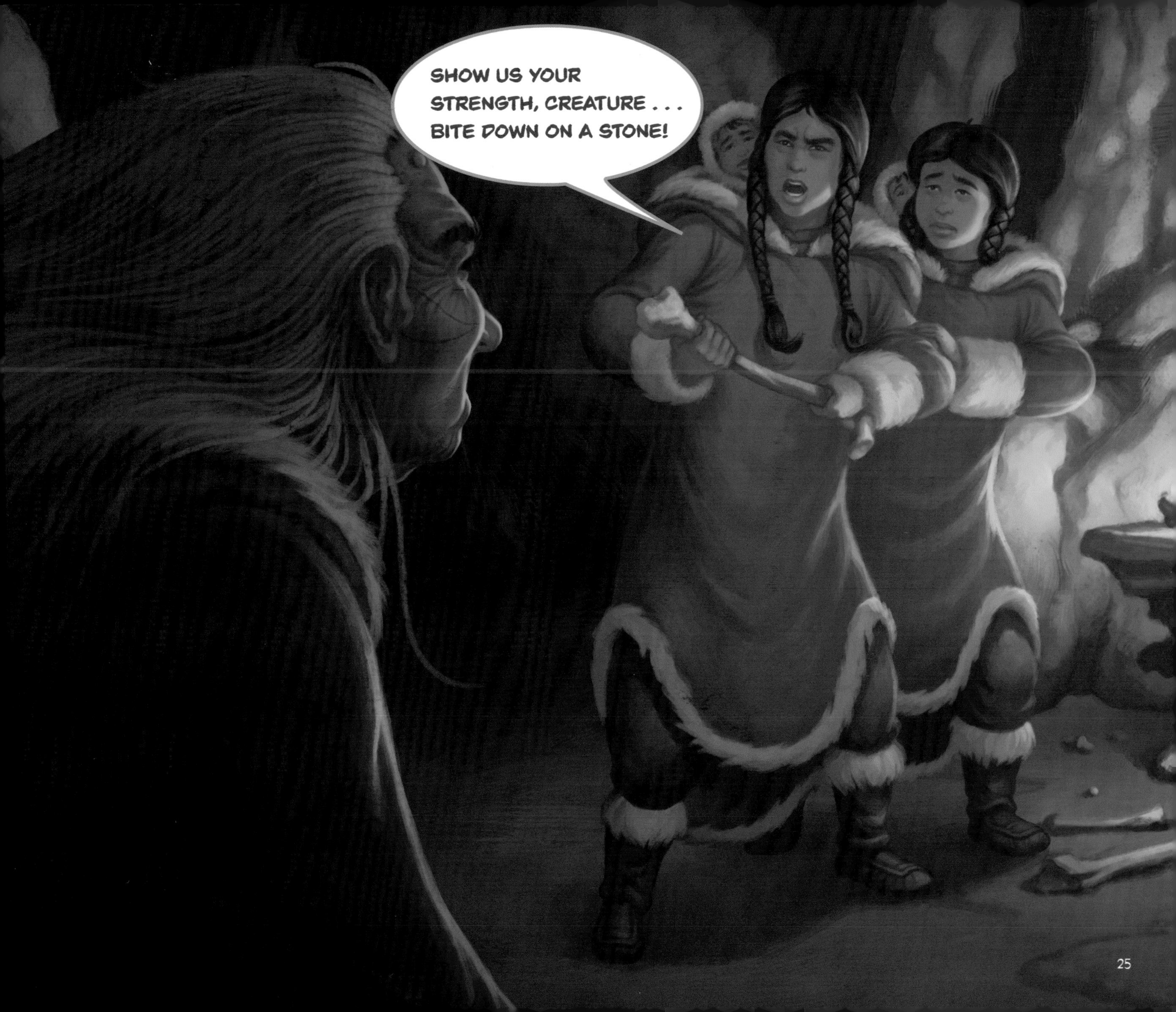
SHOW US YOUR STRENGTH, CREATURE . . . BITE DOWN ON A STONE!

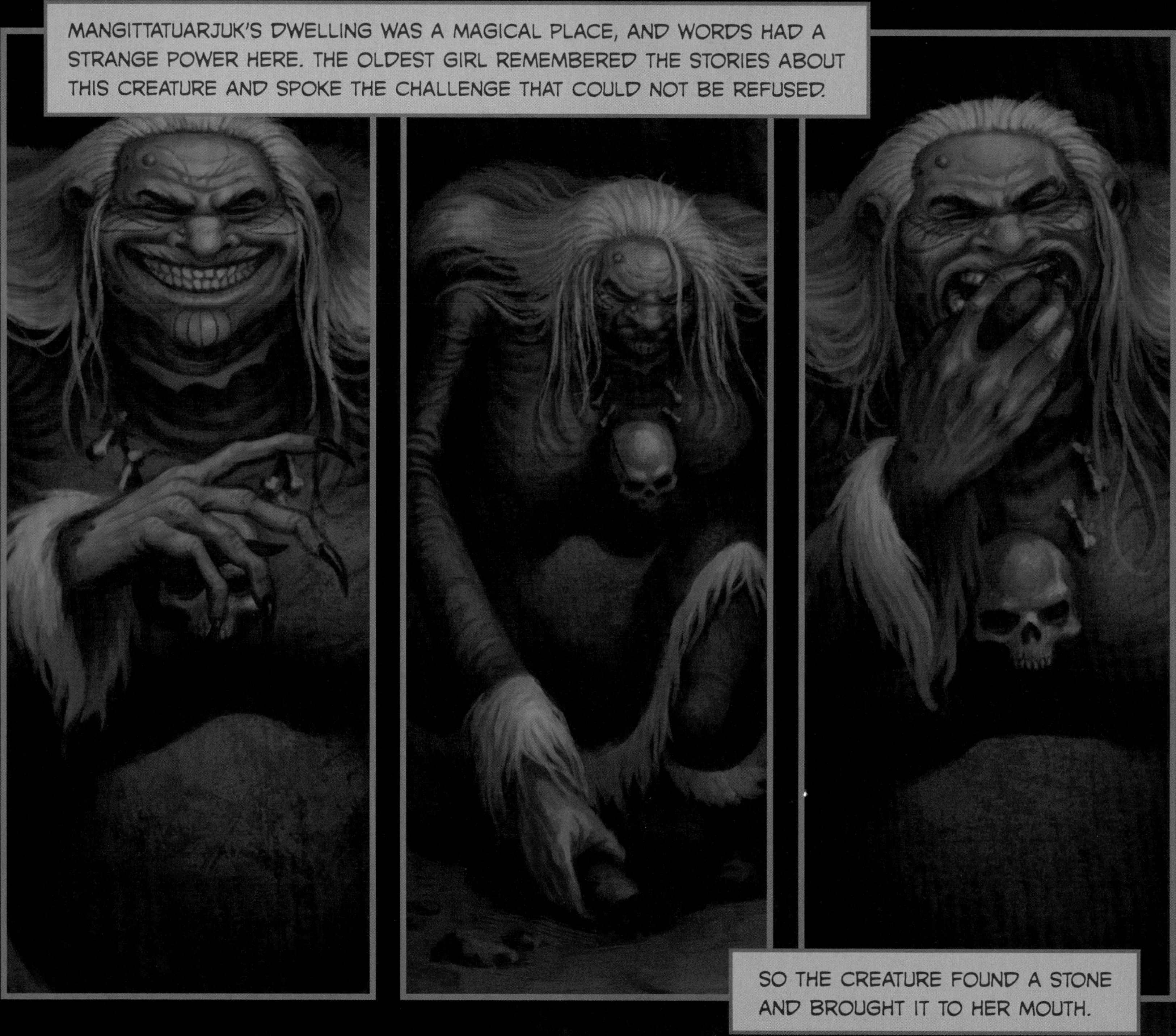
MANGITTATUARJUK'S DWELLING WAS A MAGICAL PLACE, AND WORDS HAD A STRANGE POWER HERE. THE OLDEST GIRL REMEMBERED THE STORIES ABOUT THIS CREATURE AND SPOKE THE CHALLENGE THAT COULD NOT BE REFUSED.
SO THE CREATURE FOUND A STONE AND BROUGHT IT TO HER MOUTH.

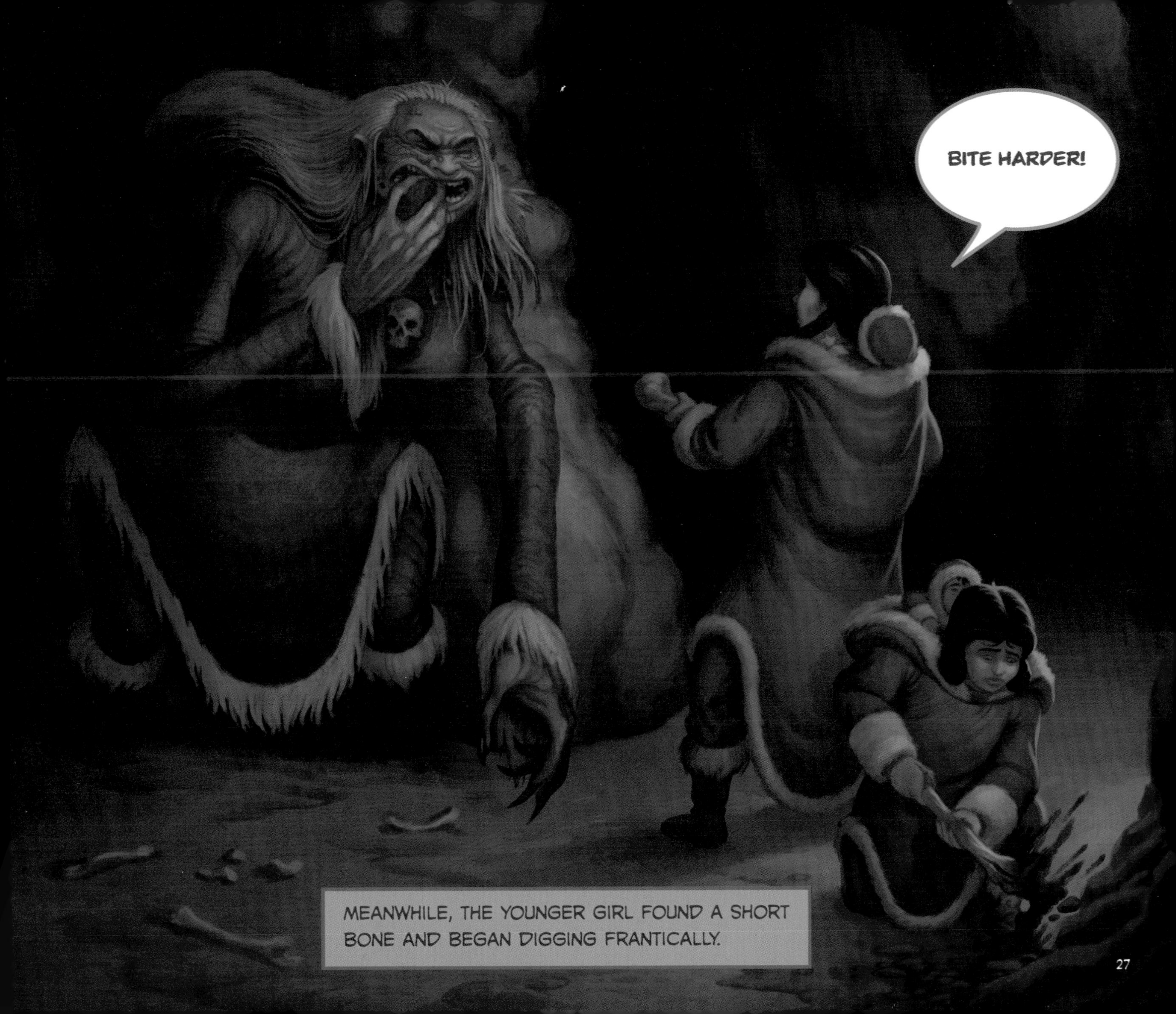
BITE HARDER!
MEANWHILE, THE YOUNGER GIRL FOUND A SHORT BONE AND BEGAN DIGGING FRANTICALLY.

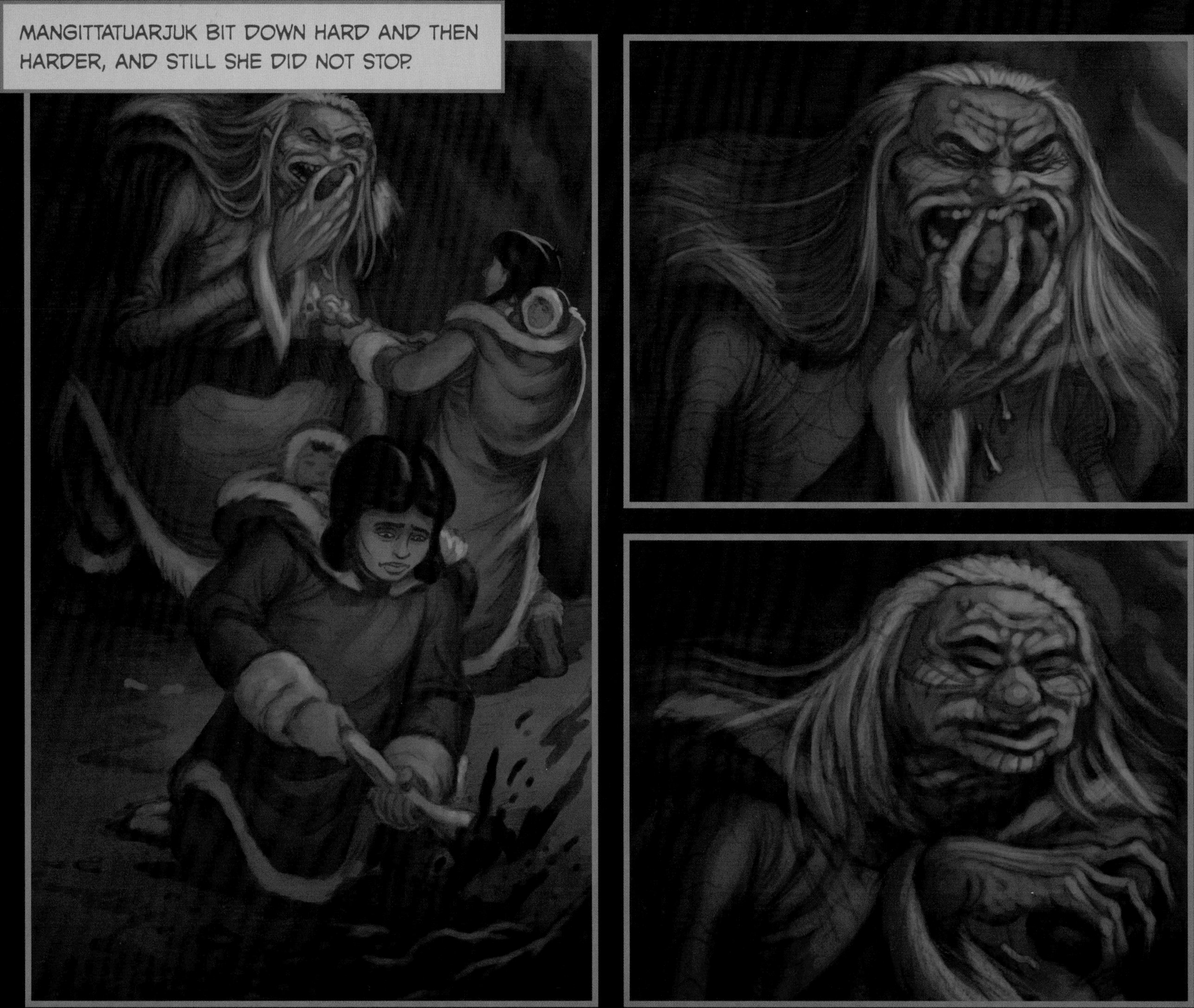
MANGITTATUARJUK BIT DOWN HARD AND THEN HARDER, AND STILL SHE DID NOT STOP.

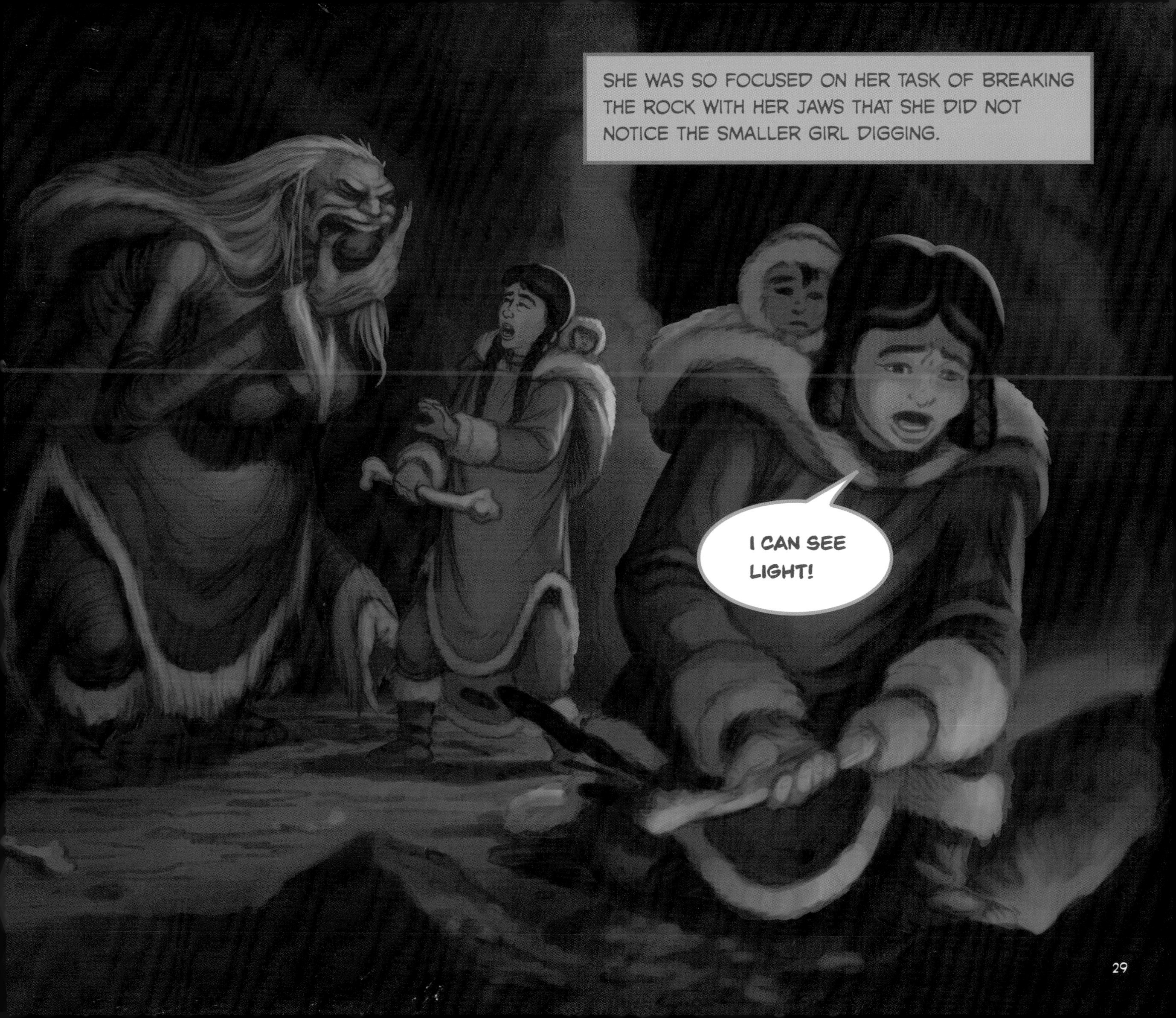
SHE WAS SO FOCUSED ON HER TASK OF BREAKING THE ROCK WITH HER JAWS THAT SHE DID NOT NOTICE THE SMALLER GIRL DIGGING.
I CAN SEE LIGHT!

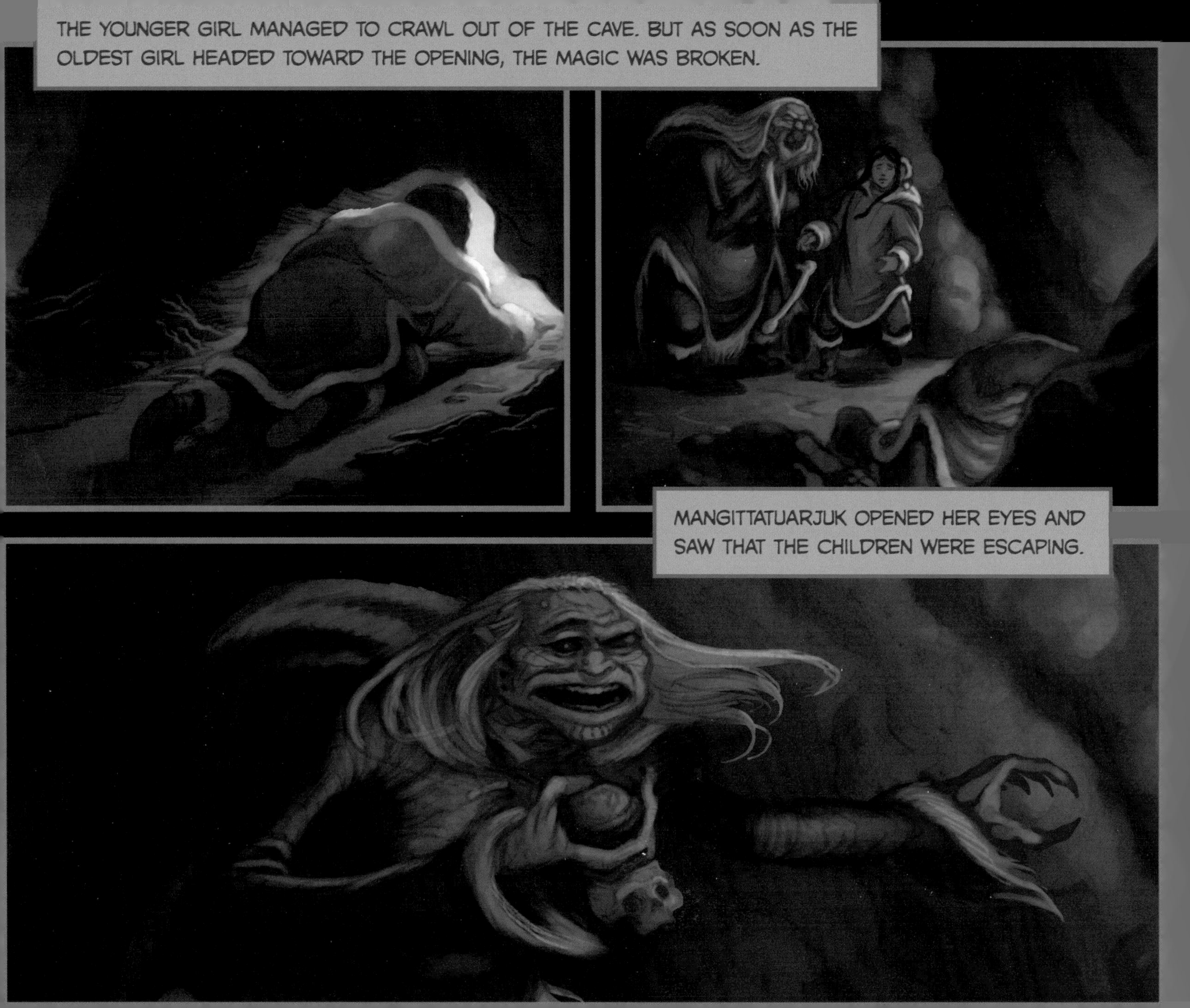
THE YOUNGER GIRL MANAGED TO CRAWL OUT OF THE CAVE. BUT AS SOON AS THE OLDEST GIRL HEADED TOWARD THE OPENING, THE MAGIC WAS BROKEN.
MANGITTATUARJUK OPENED HER EYES AND SAW THAT THE CHILDREN WERE ESCAPING.

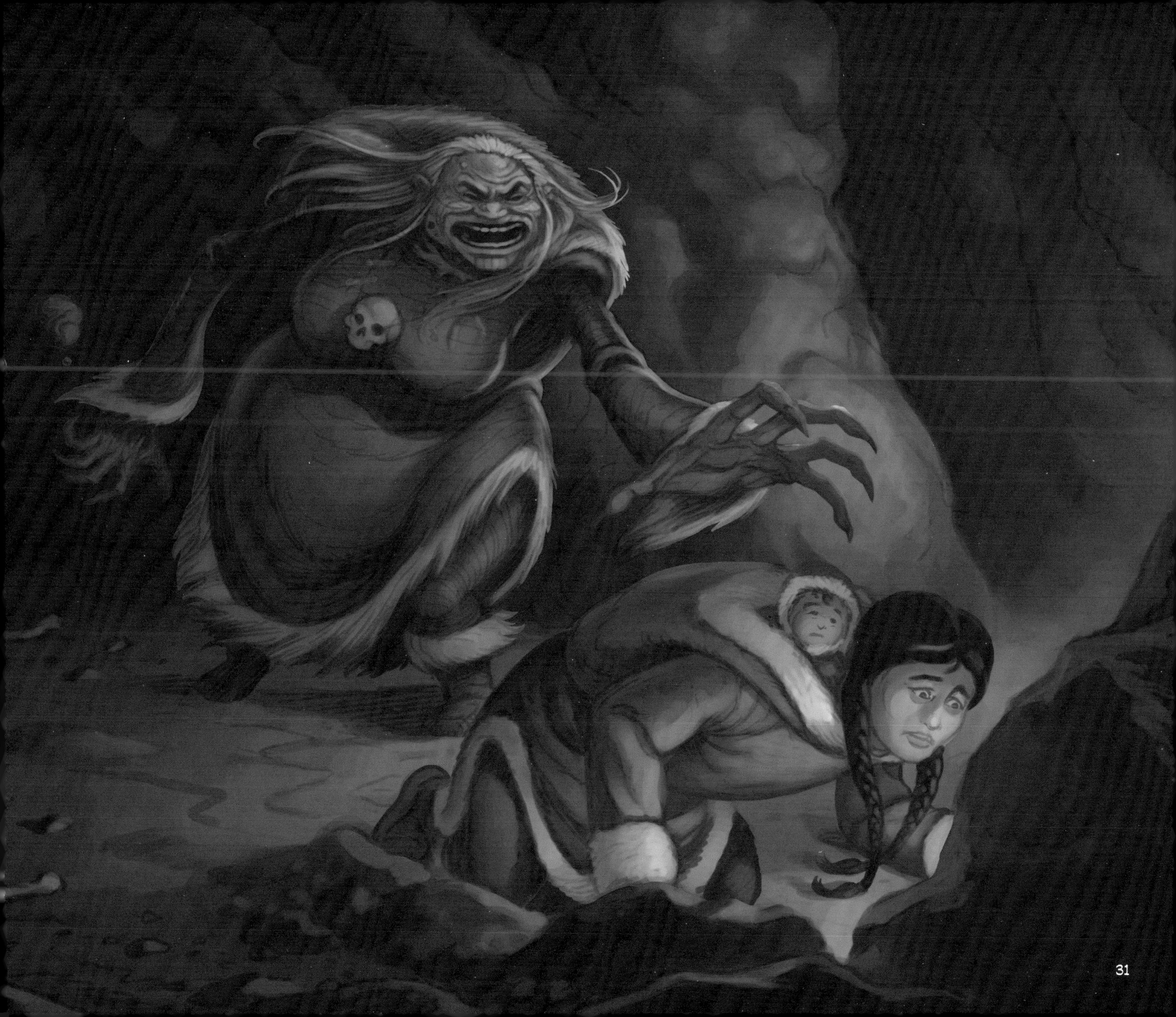

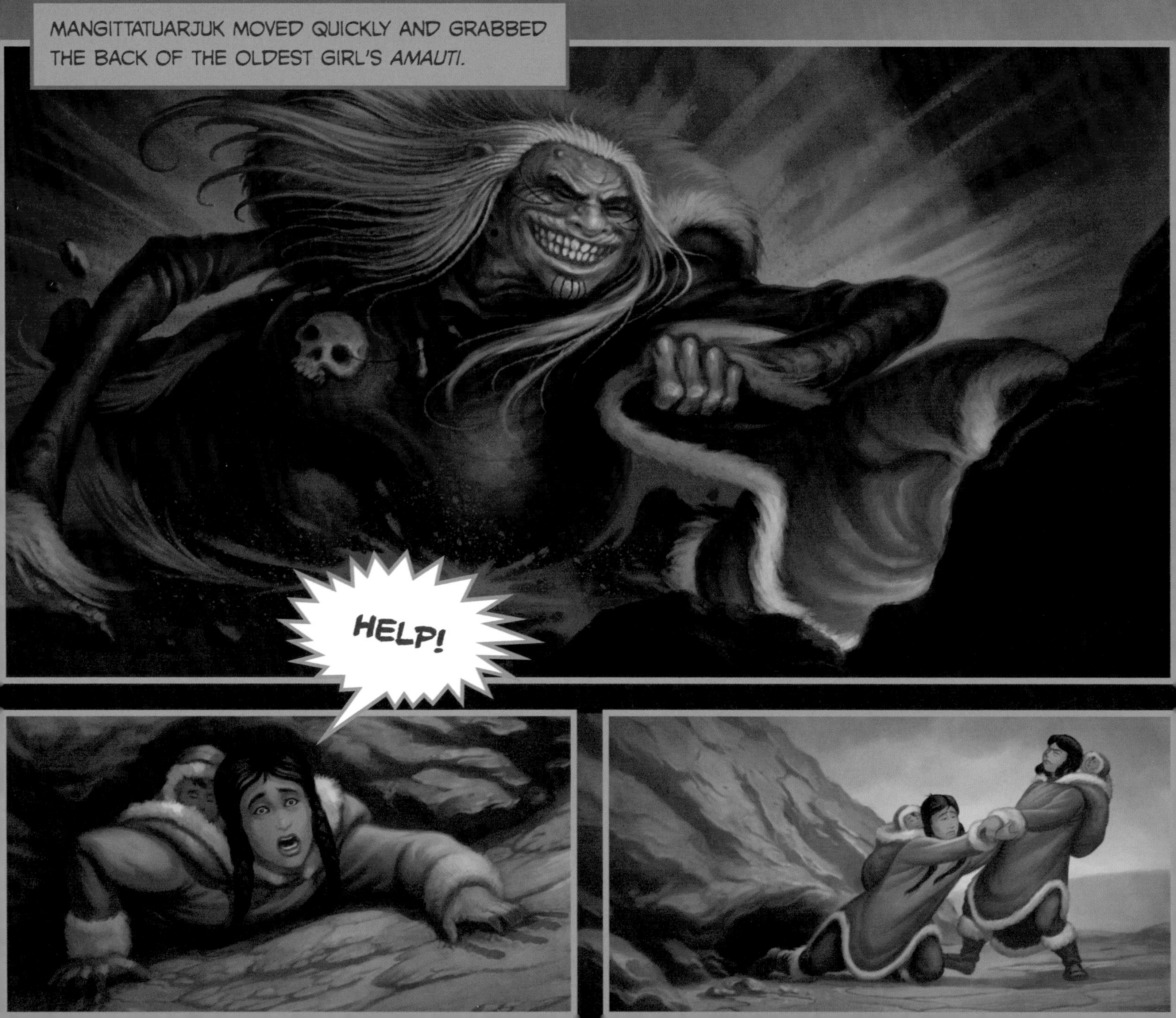
MANGITTATUARJUK MOVED QUICKLY AND GRABBED THE BACK OF THE OLDEST GIRL'S *AMAUTI*.
HELP!

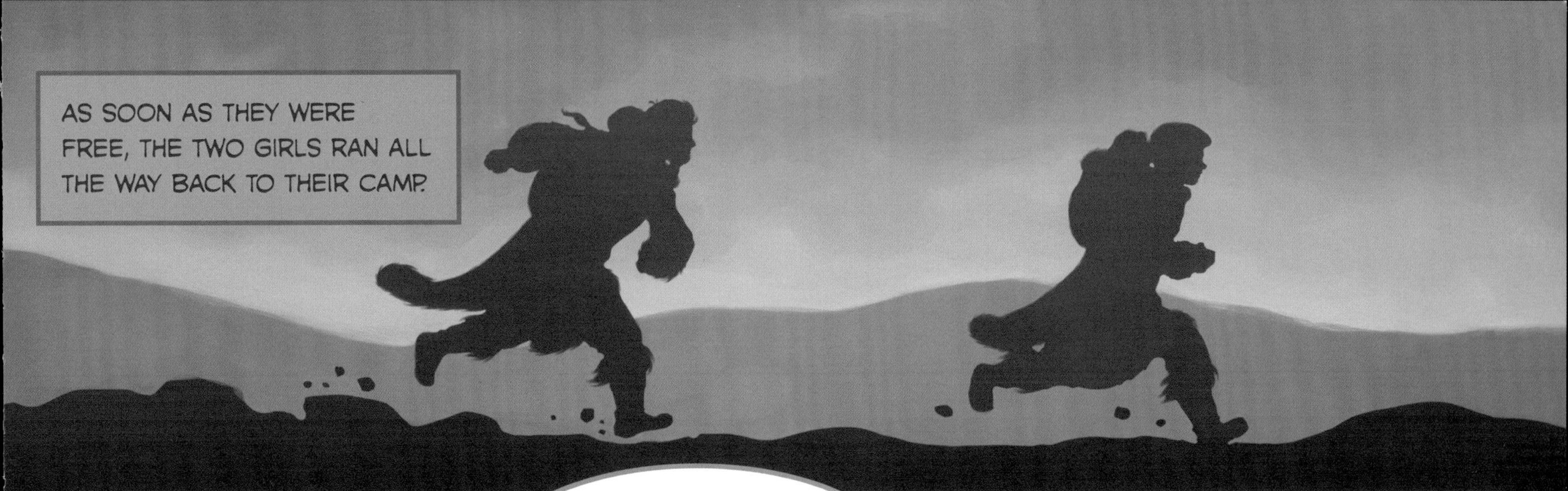
AS SOON AS THEY WERE FREE, THE TWO GIRLS RAN ALL THE WAY BACK TO THEIR CAMP.

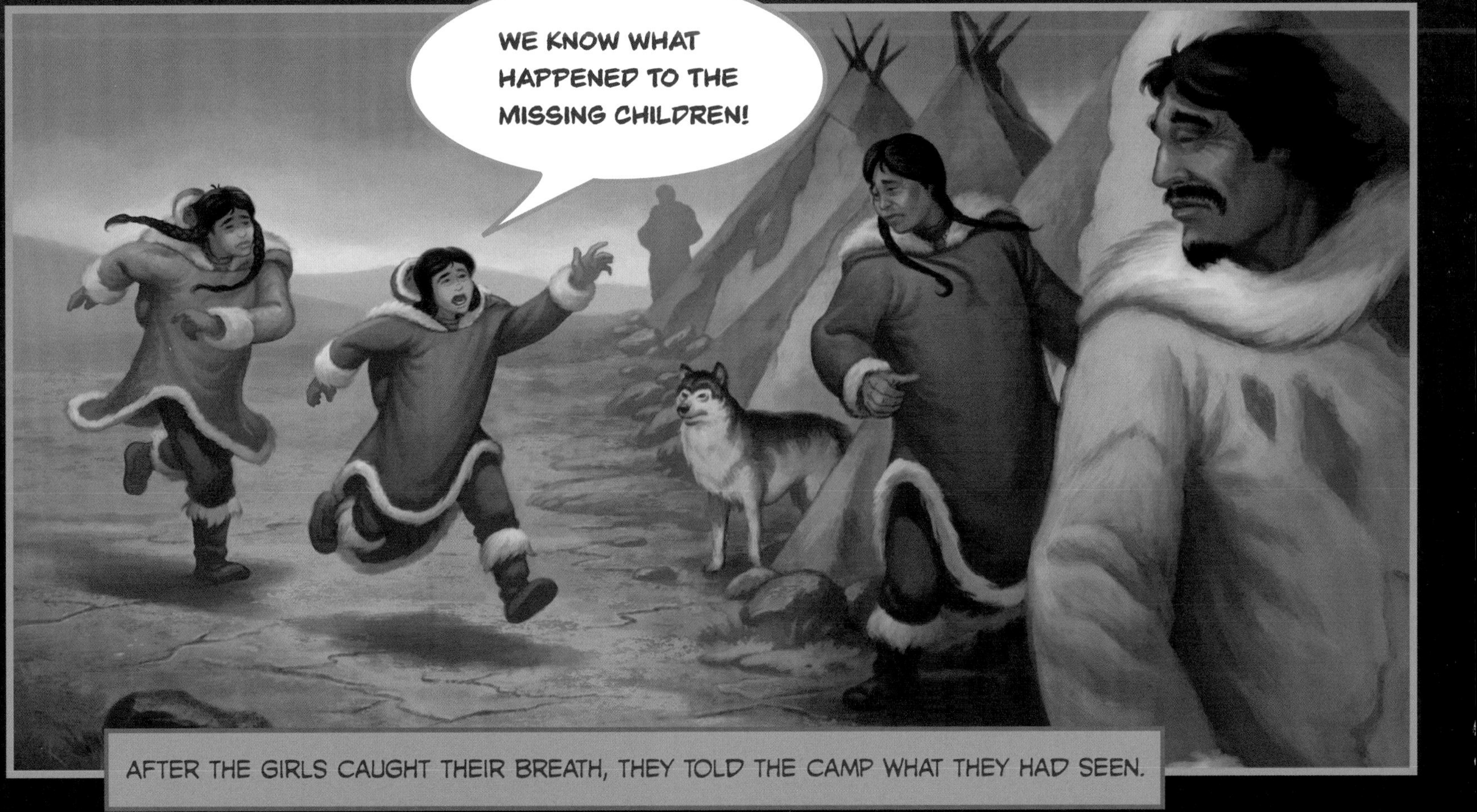
WE KNOW WHAT HAPPENED TO THE MISSING CHILDREN!
AFTER THE GIRLS CAUGHT THEIR BREATH, THEY TOLD THE CAMP WHAT THEY HAD SEEN.

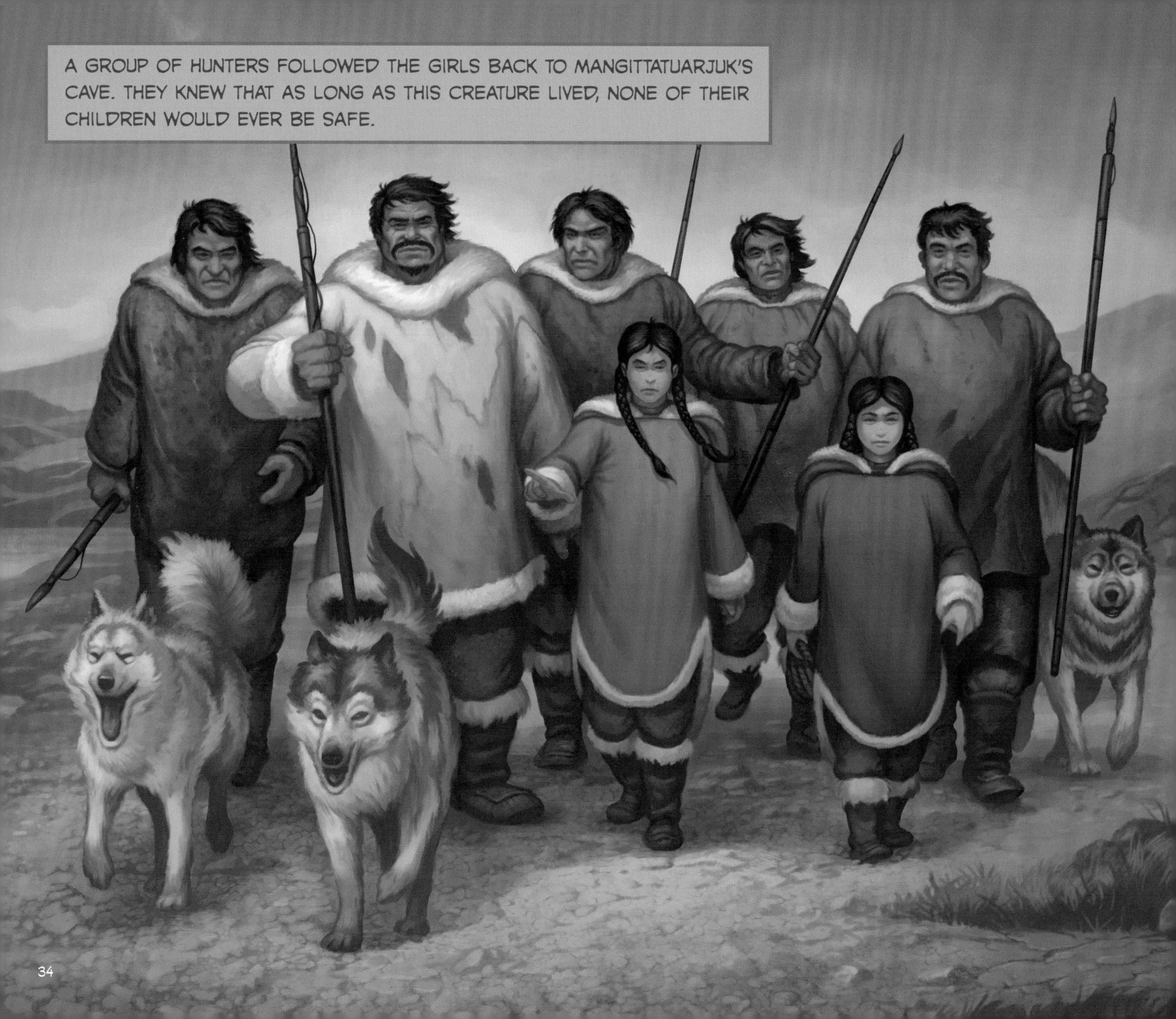
A GROUP OF HUNTERS FOLLOWED THE GIRLS BACK TO MANGITTATUARJUK'S CAVE. THEY KNEW THAT AS LONG AS THIS CREATURE LIVED, NONE OF THEIR CHILDREN WOULD EVER BE SAFE.

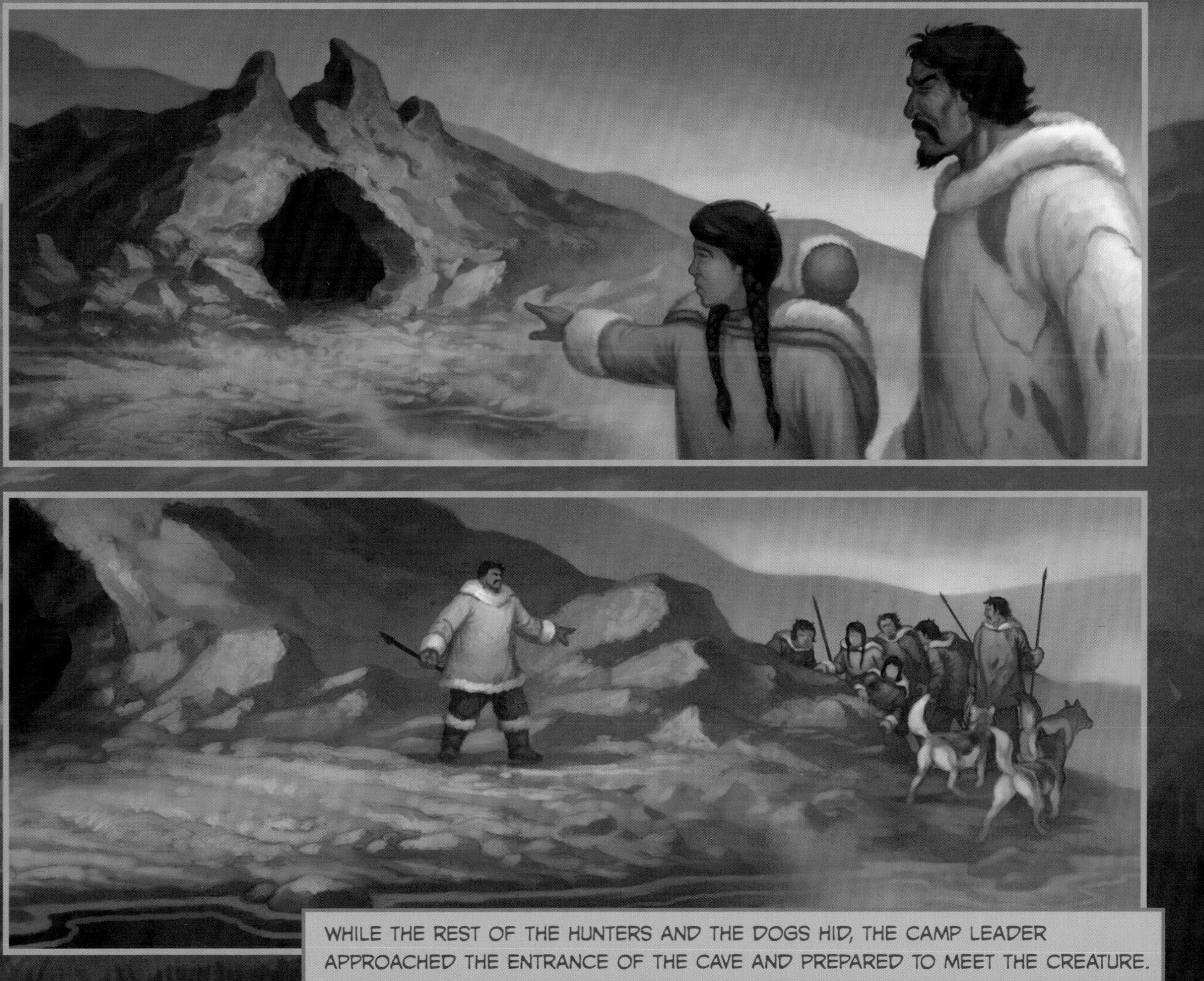
WHILE THE REST OF THE HUNTERS AND THE DOGS HID, THE CAMP LEADER APPROACHED THE ENTRANCE OF THE CAVE AND PREPARED TO MEET THE CREATURE.

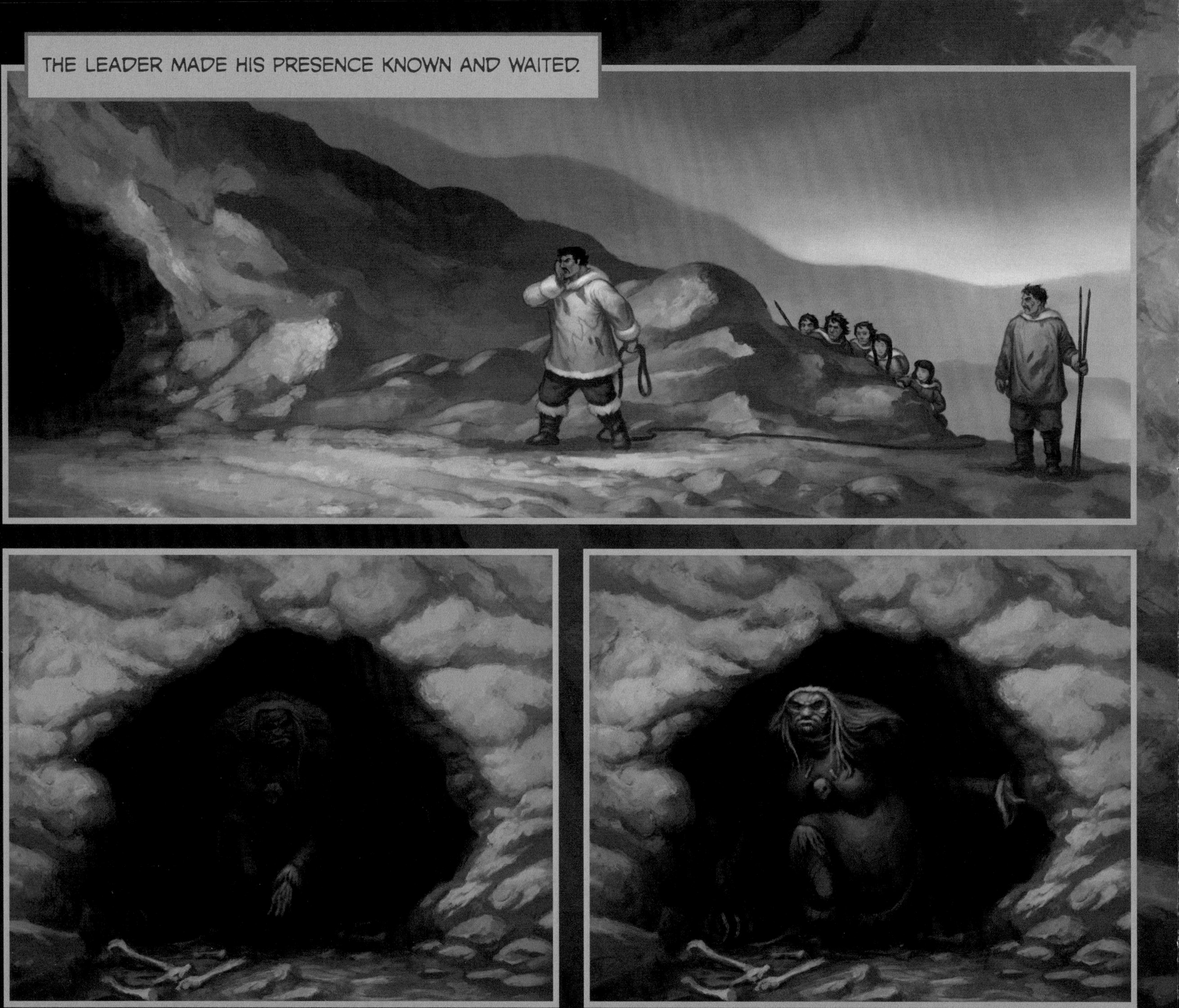
THE LEADER MADE HIS PRESENCE KNOWN AND WAITED.

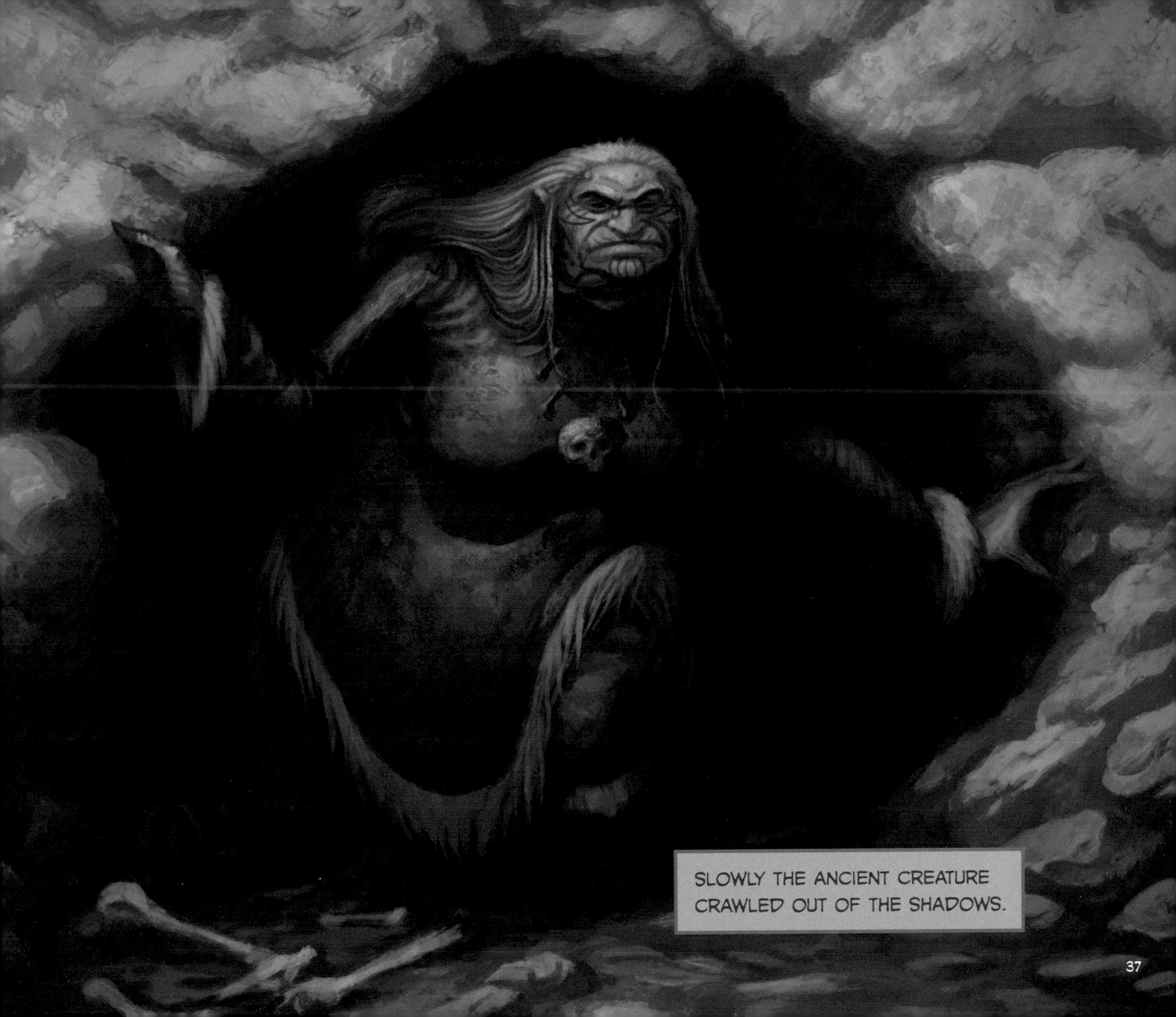
SLOWLY THE ANCIENT CREATURE CRAWLED OUT OF THE SHADOWS.

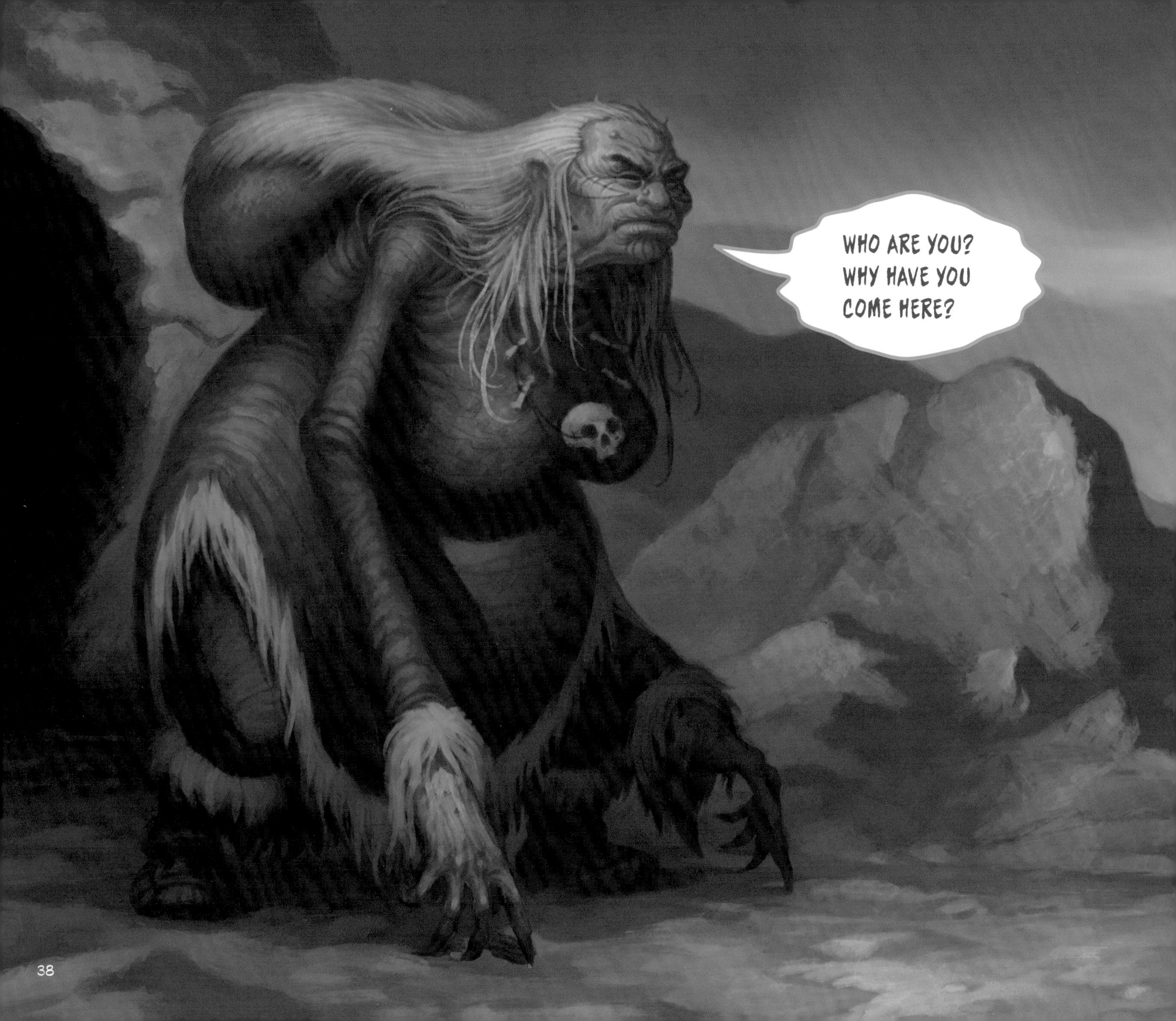
WHO ARE YOU?
WHY HAVE YOU
COME HERE?

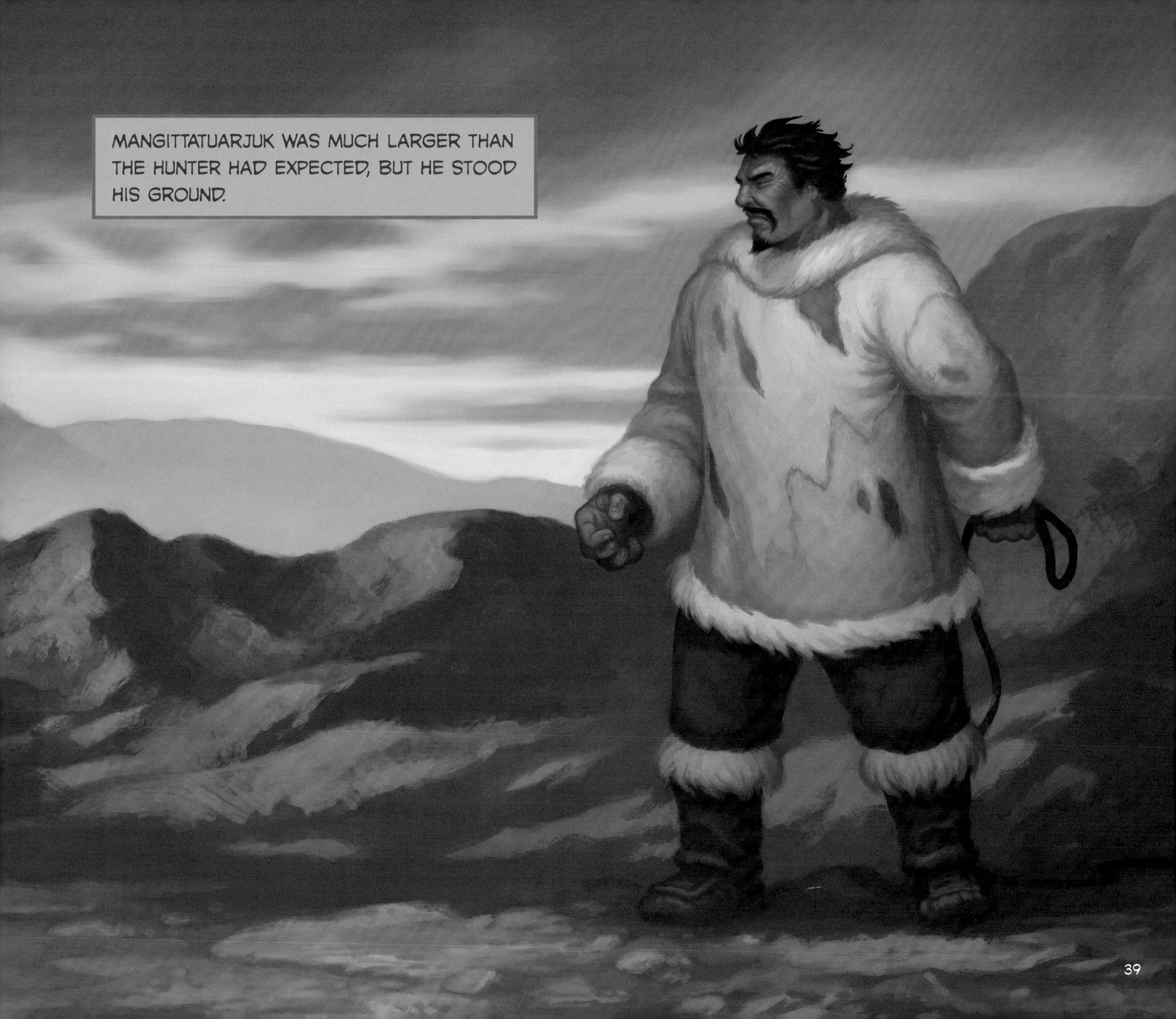
MANGITTATUARJUK WAS MUCH LARGER THAN THE HUNTER HAD EXPECTED, BUT HE STOOD HIS GROUND.

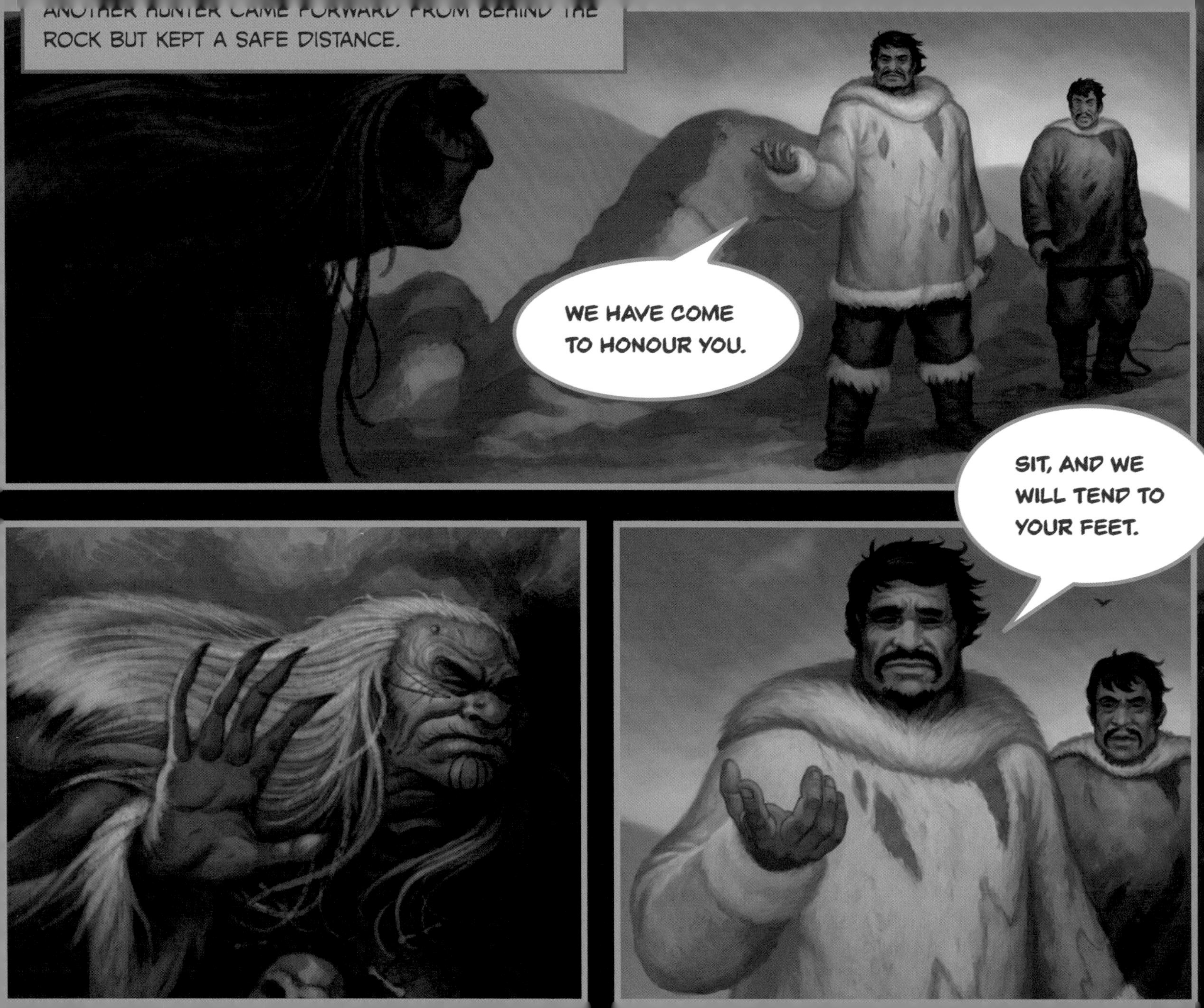
ANOTHER HUNTER CAME FORWARD FROM BEHIND THE ROCK BUT KEPT A SAFE DISTANCE.
WE HAVE COME TO HONOUR YOU.
SIT, AND WE WILL TEND TO YOUR FEET.

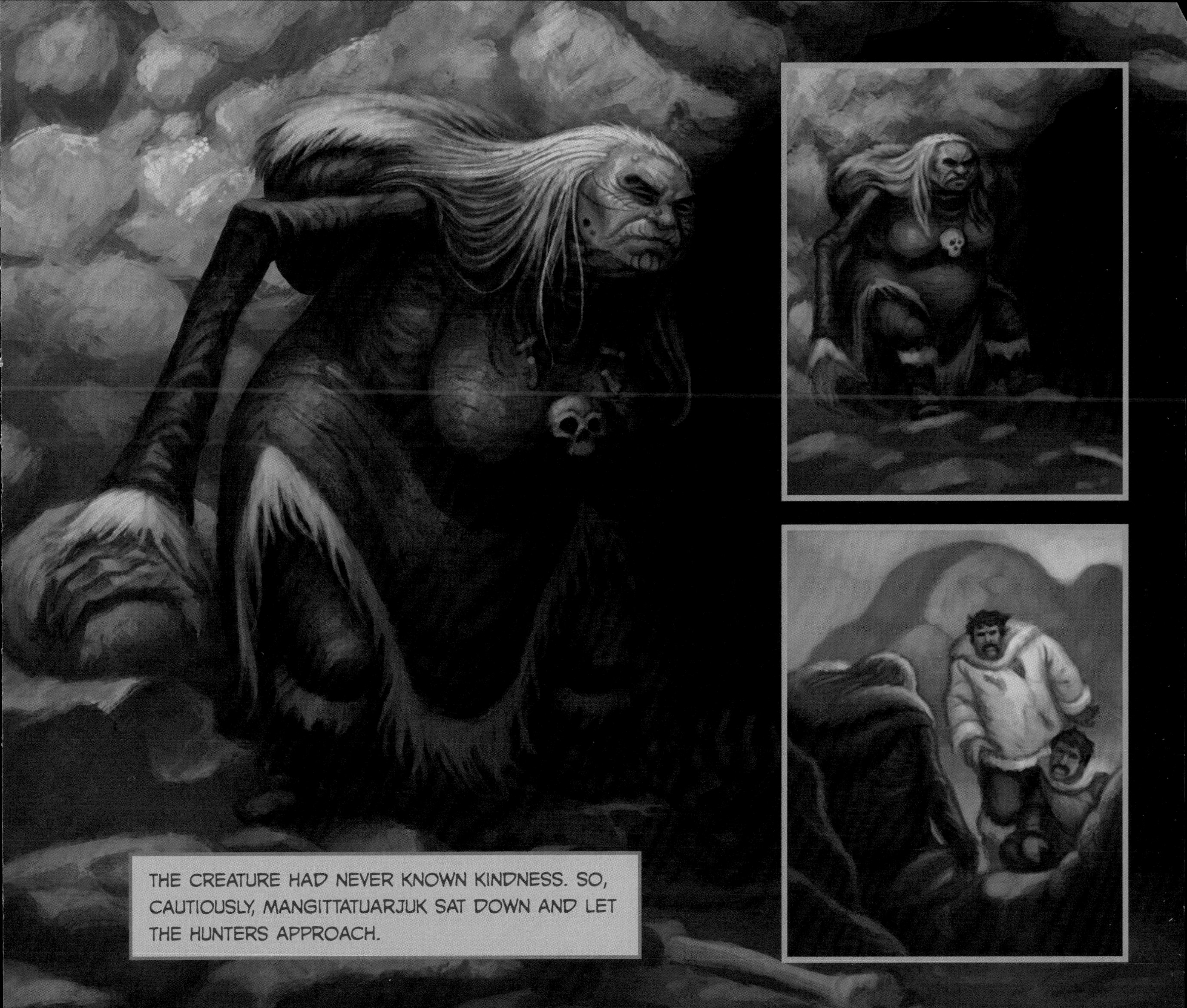
THE CREATURE HAD NEVER KNOWN KINDNESS. SO, CAUTIOUSLY, MANGITTATUARJUK SAT DOWN AND LET THE HUNTERS APPROACH.

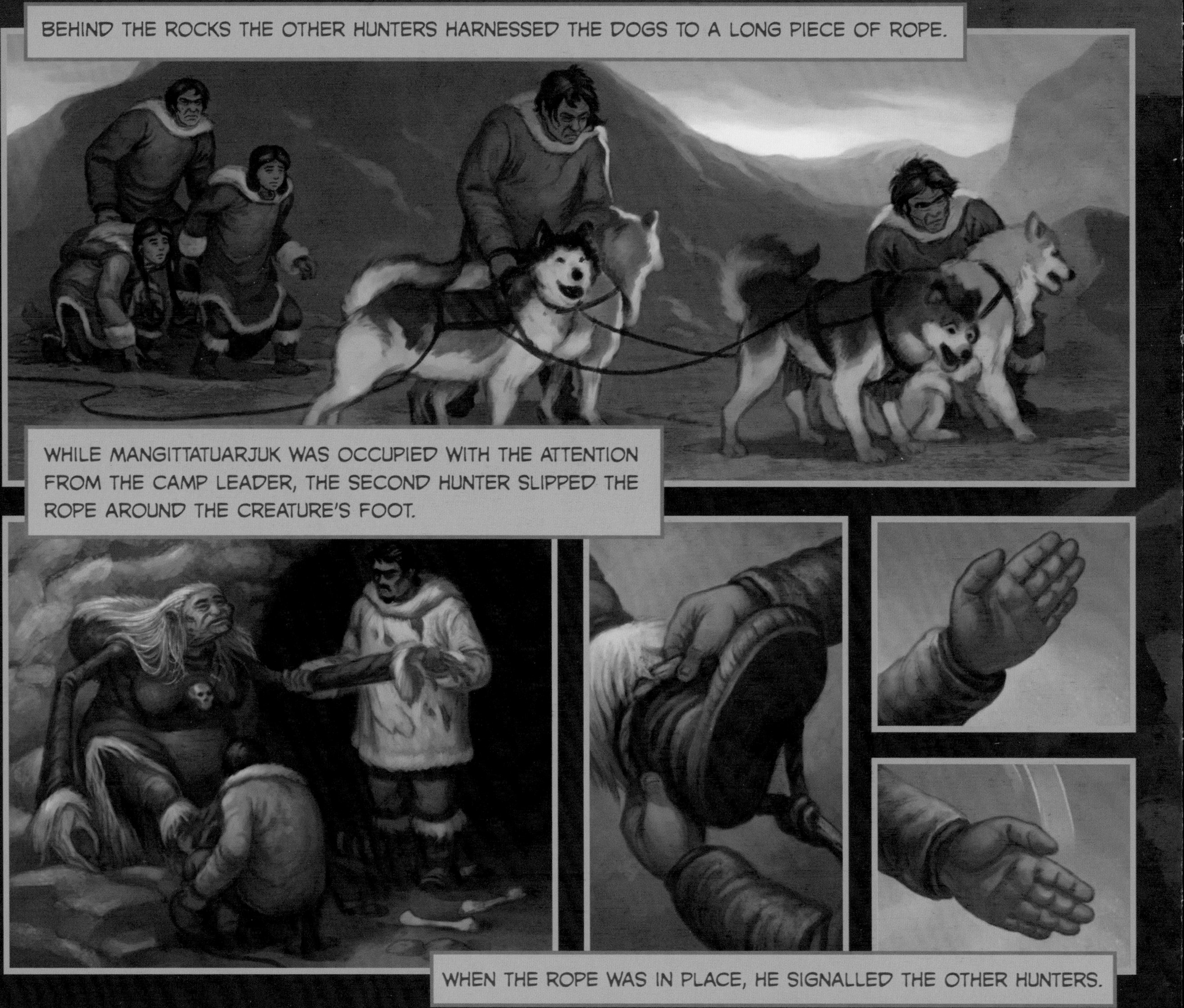
BEHIND THE ROCKS THE OTHER HUNTERS HARNESSED THE DOGS TO A LONG PIECE OF ROPE.
WHILE MANGITTATUARJUK WAS OCCUPIED WITH THE ATTENTION FROM THE CAMP LEADER, THE SECOND HUNTER SLIPPED THE ROPE AROUND THE CREATURE'S FOOT.
WHEN THE ROPE WAS IN PLACE, HE SIGNALLED THE OTHER HUNTERS.

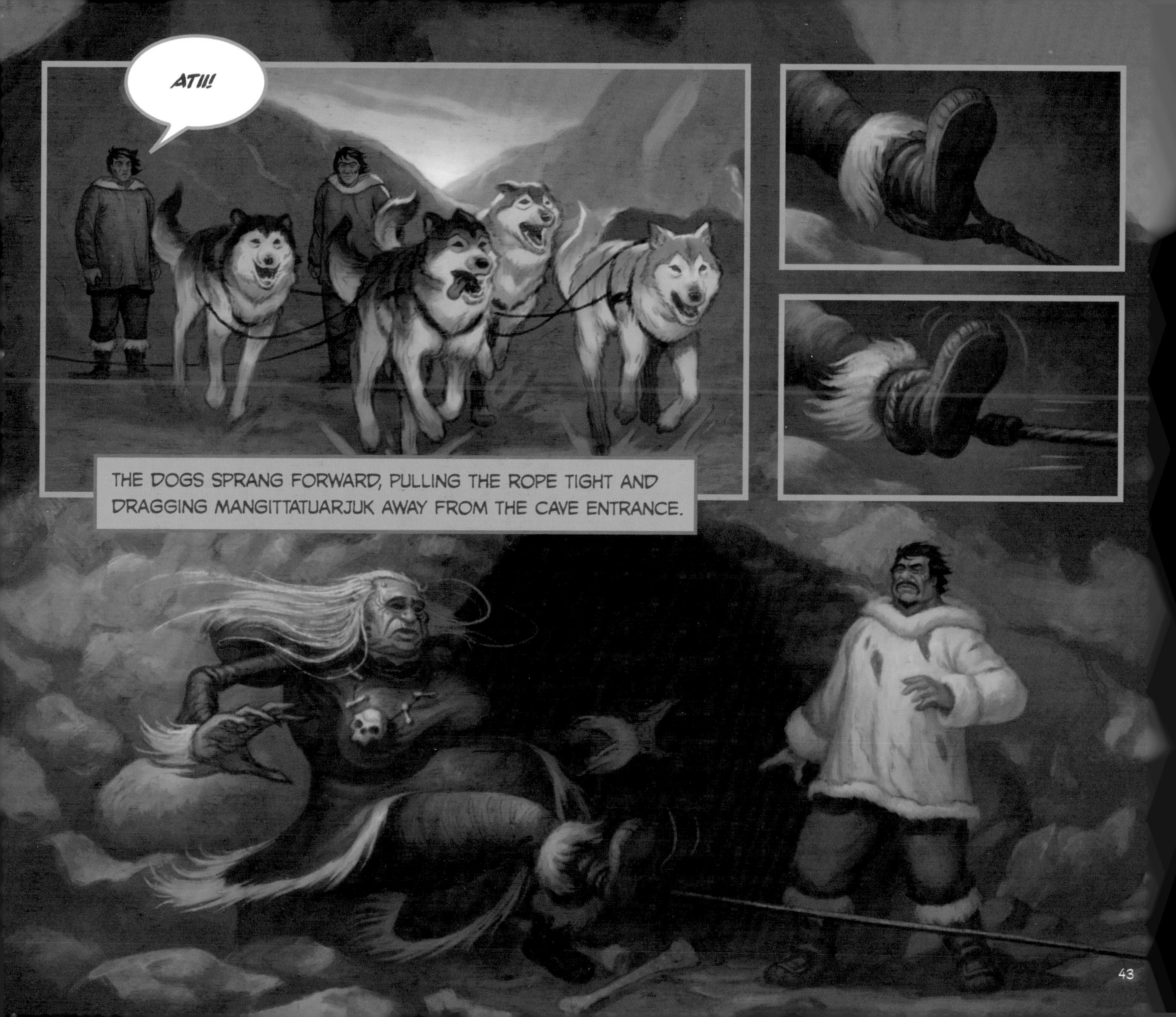

ATII!
THE DOGS SPRANG FORWARD, PULLING THE ROPE TIGHT AND DRAGGING MANGITTATUARJUK AWAY FROM THE CAVE ENTRANCE.

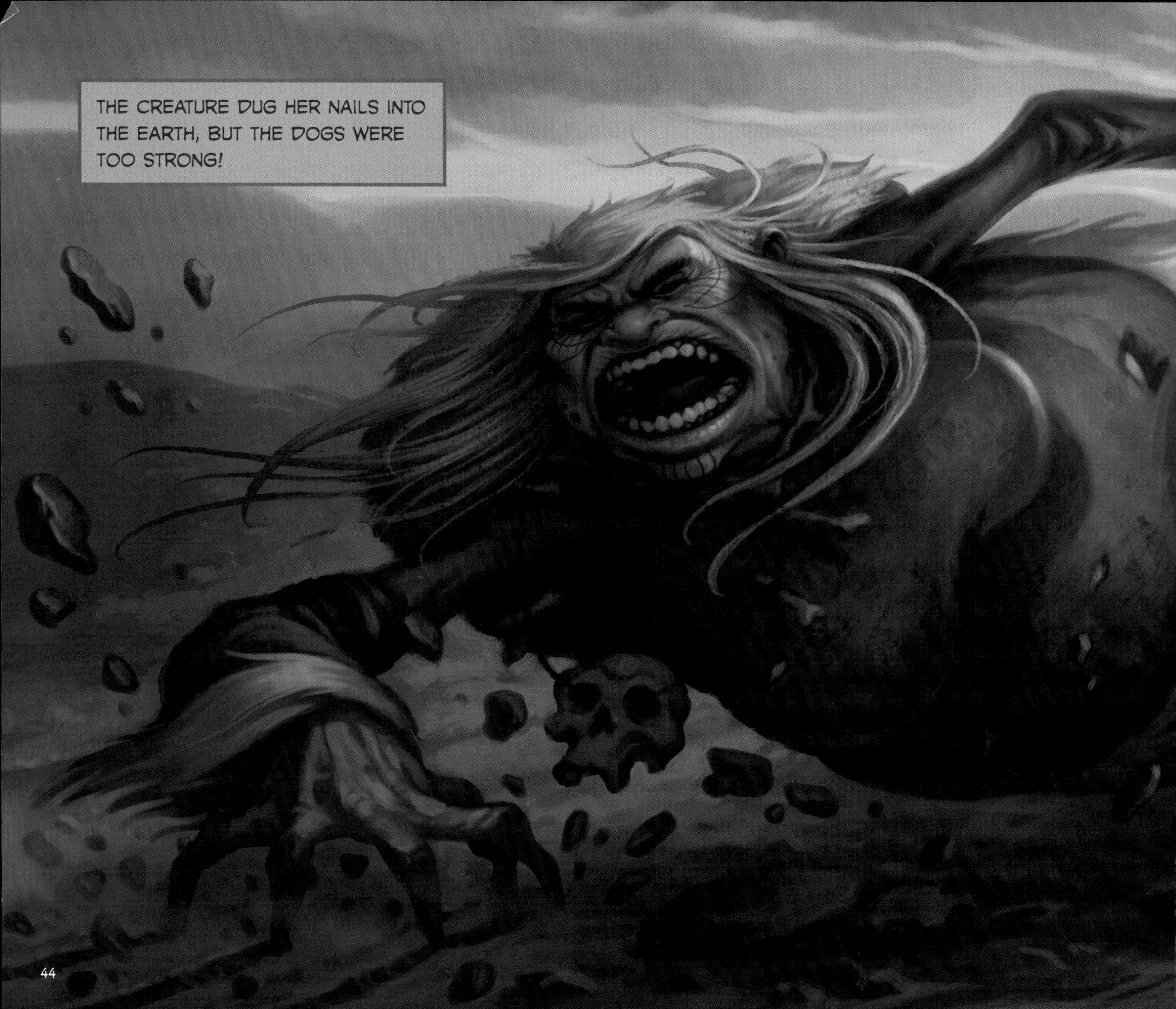
THE CREATURE DUG HER NAILS INTO THE EARTH, BUT THE DOGS WERE TOO STRONG!

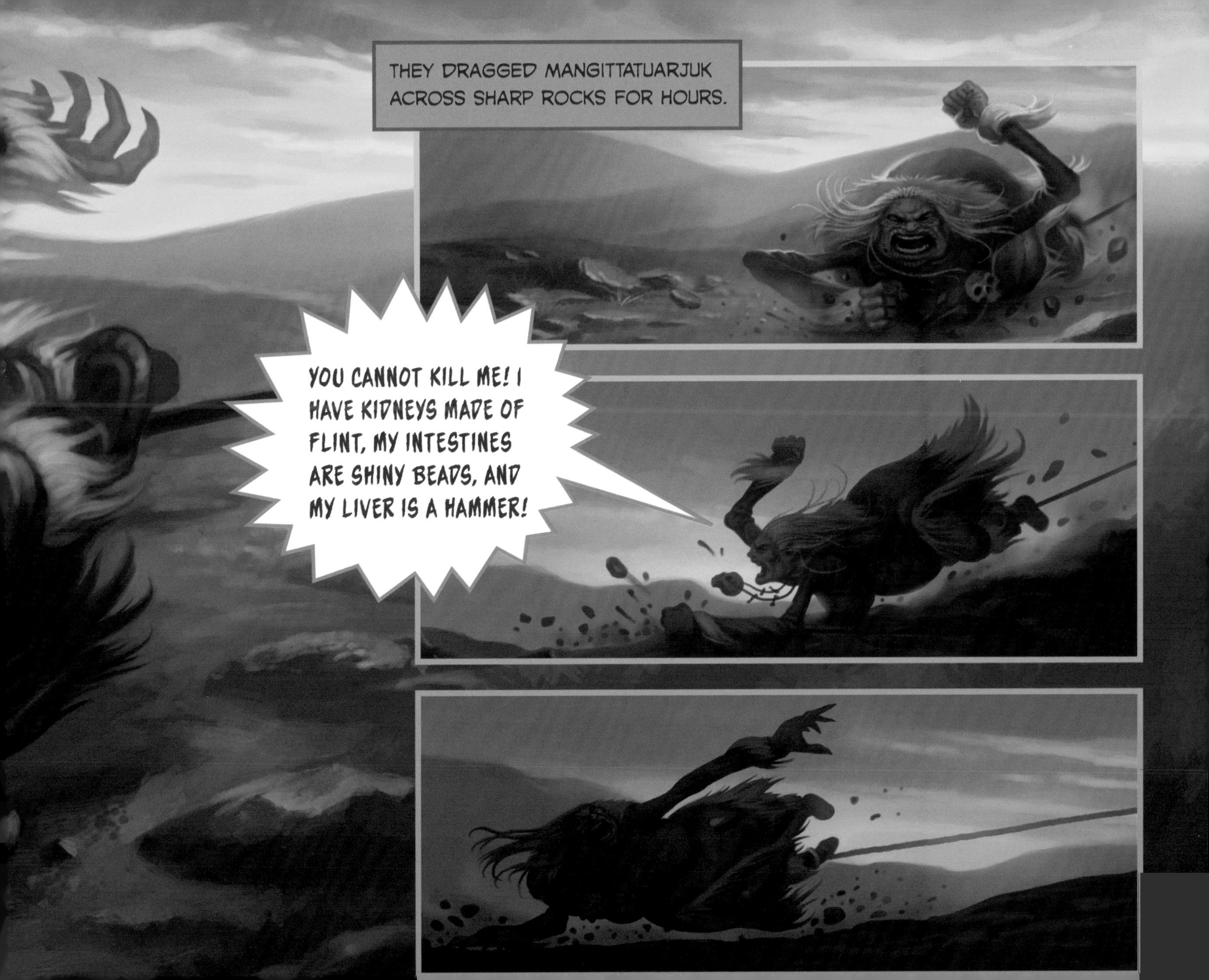
THEY DRAGGED MANGITTATUARJUK ACROSS SHARP ROCKS FOR HOURS.
YOU CANNOT KILL ME! I HAVE KIDNEYS MADE OF FLINT, MY INTESTINES ARE SHINY BEADS, AND MY LIVER IS A HAMMER!

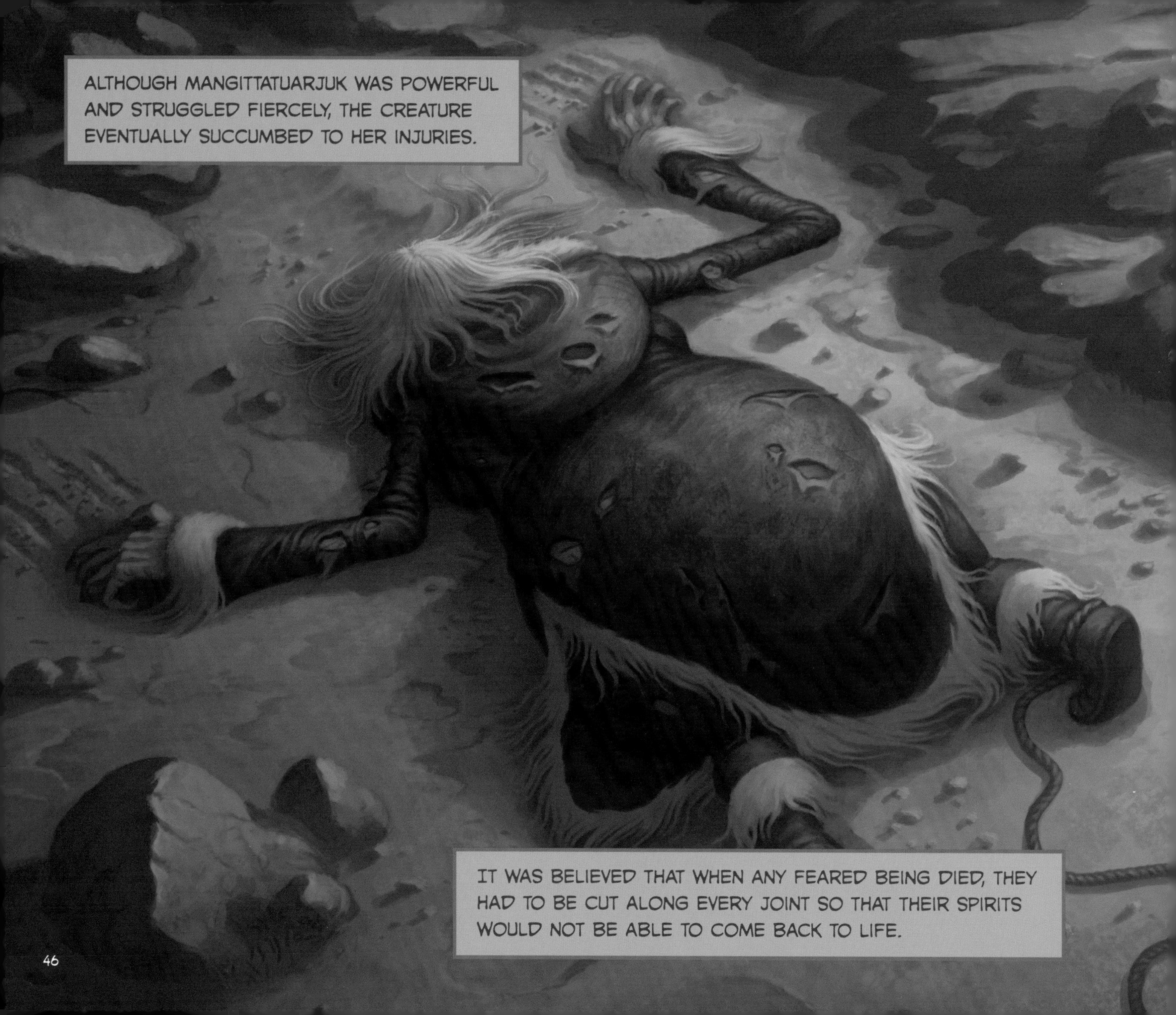
ALTHOUGH MANGITTATUARJUK WAS POWERFUL AND STRUGGLED FIERCELY, THE CREATURE EVENTUALLY SUCCUMBED TO HER INJURIES.
IT WAS BELIEVED THAT WHEN ANY FEARED BEING DIED, THEY HAD TO BE CUT ALONG EVERY JOINT SO THAT THEIR SPIRITS WOULD NOT BE ABLE TO COME BACK TO LIFE.

SURE ENOUGH, AS SHE HAD SAID, HER KIDNEYS WERE MADE OF FLINT, HER INTESTINES WERE BEAUTIFUL BEAD AND HER LIVER WAS A HAMMER.

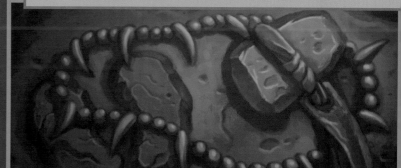

THE HUNTERS BROUGHT THE FLINT, THE BEADS, AND THE HAMME HOME. BUT WHEN THEY WOKE UP THE NEXT MORNING, THE ITEMS HAD TURNED INTO KIDNEYS, INTESTINES, AND A LIVER.

AND SO, MANGITTATUARJUK, BEING A SUPERNATURAL CREATURE, WAS CUT UP INTO PIECES AT EVERY JOINT OF HER BODY.

AND THAT IS THE LEGEND OF MANGITTATUARJUK, THE GNAWER OF ROCKS!

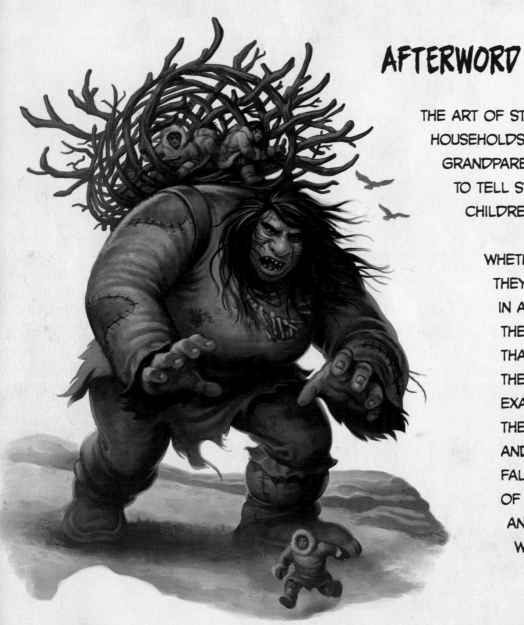

AFTERWORD

THE ART OF STORYTELLING IS NOW QUITE RARE IN HOUSEHOLDS WHEN ONCE IT WAS THE NORM FOR GRANDPARENTS, PARENTS, AUNTS, AND UNCLES TO TELL STORIES IN THE EVENINGS TO ENTERTAIN CHILDREN.

WHETHER THE STORIES WERE TRUE OR NOT, THEY WERE USED TO EDUCATE CHILDREN IN A WAY THAT THEY COULD REMEMBER. THEY WARNED OF DANGEROUS THINGS THAT COULD HAPPEN IN REAL LIFE. THE STORIES OF *QALUPALIIT*, FOR EXAMPLE, KEPT CHILDREN AWAY FROM THE PRESSURE RIDGES, CRACKS, AND LEADS SO THAT THEY WOULDN'T FALL IN AND DROWN. THE STORIES OF MANGITTATUARJUK, *AMAUTALIIT*, AND OTHER LAND-DWELLING BEINGS WERE TOLD SO CHILDREN WOULD

NOT WANDER OFF TOO FAR FROM CAMP AND FROM THE PROTECTION OF THEIR PARENTS AS THEY COULD BECOME PREY TO THE BIGGEST CARNIVORES ON THE PLANET . . . POLAR BEARS. A LOT OF THE STORIES ALSO HAVE ILL-TREATED ORPHANS AND OLD LADIES. THESE WERE MORAL STORIES OF HOW NOT TO TREAT THOSE LESS FORTUNATE AS ONE CAN EASILY END UP LIKE THEM.

TODAY, WITH TECHNOLOGY AND SO MANY GADGETS THAT CHILDREN NOW HAVE ACCESS TO, THEY ARE NOT EXPOSED TO THE STORIES THAT OUR PARENTS WERE. MY GRANDPARENTS WOULD HAVE BEEN TOLD ORAL TRADITIONS IN *QARMAIT*, AND MY PARENTS IN HOUSES THE SIZE OF SHACKS. FORTY YEARS AGO, WE WERE TOLD THESE STORIES IN A SCHOOL BY ELDERS SUCH AS LEVI IQALUGJUAQ. TODAY, CHILDREN ARE LUCKY IF AN ELDER CAN TELL THESE STORIES IN A CLASSROOM. THAT IS WHY IT IS SO IMPORTANT TO CAPTURE THESE STORIES IN PRINT.

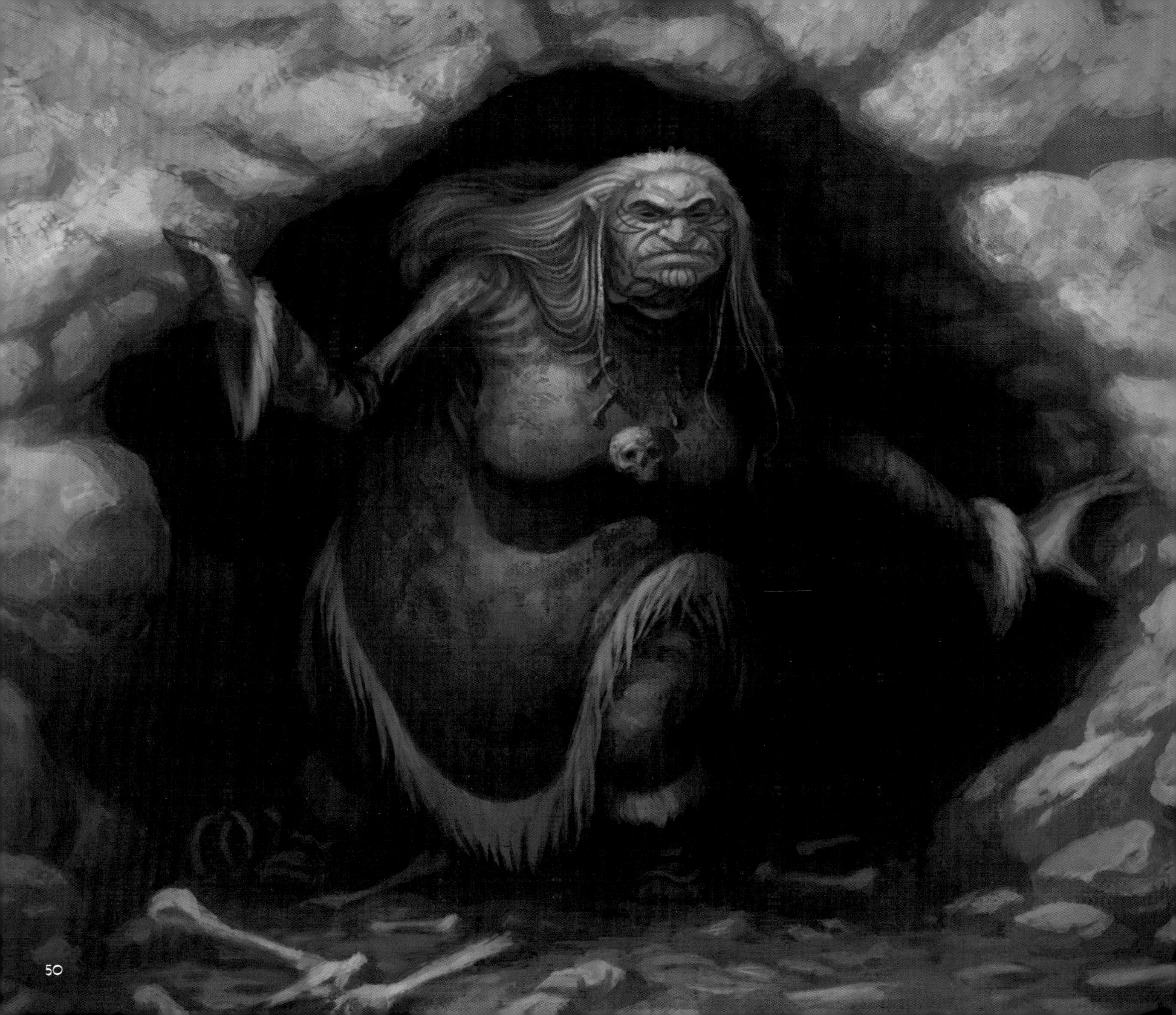

GLOSSARY

AMAUTALIIT	[A-MOW-TA-LEET]	OGRESSES WHO WANDER THE TUNDRA LOOKING FOR CHILDREN TO SNATCH.
AMAUTI	[A-MOW-TEE]	A WOMAN'S PARKA—USUALLY WITH A POUCH IN THE HOOD TO CARRY A BABY.
ATII	[A-TEE]	"LET'S GO!"
MANGITTATUARJUK	[MAN-GET-TAT-TOW-A-YUK]	NAME, MEANING "GNAWER."
QALUPALIIT	[KA-LOO-PA-LEET]	WATER CREATURES WHO KIDNAP CHILDREN PLAYING TOO CLOSE TO ICE CRACKS AND PULL THEM UNDERWATER.
QARMAIT	[KAR-MATE]	SOD HOUSES.

LOUISE FLAHERTY

LOUISE FLAHERTY GREW UP IN CLYDE RIVER, NUNAVUT. EARLY ON, LOUISE WAS FORTUNATE TO BE SURROUNDED BY GREAT STORYTELLERS. HER GRANDPARENTS INSTILLED IN HER A PASSION FOR INUKTITUT AND AN UNDERSTANDING THAT SPEAKING INUKTITUT IS A FUNDAMENTAL PART OF INUIT IDENTITY. IN 2005, LOUISE CO-FOUNDED INHABIT MEDIA INC., AN INDEPENDENT PUBLISHING HOUSE DEDICATED TO THE PRESERVATION AND PROMOTION OF INUIT KNOWLEDGE AND VALUES, AND THE INUKTITUT LANGUAGE. INHABIT MEDIA HAS SINCE PUBLISHED DOZENS OF BOOKS AND INUKTITUT RESOURCES THAT ARE USED IN CLASSROOMS THROUGHOUT NUNAVUT.

JIM NELSON

JIM NELSON IS A FREELANCE ARTIST BASED IN CHICAGO, ILLINOIS. HE HAS A LIFELONG INTEREST IN MYTHS, LEGENDS, AND THE FANTASTIC.

INHABIT
MEDIA

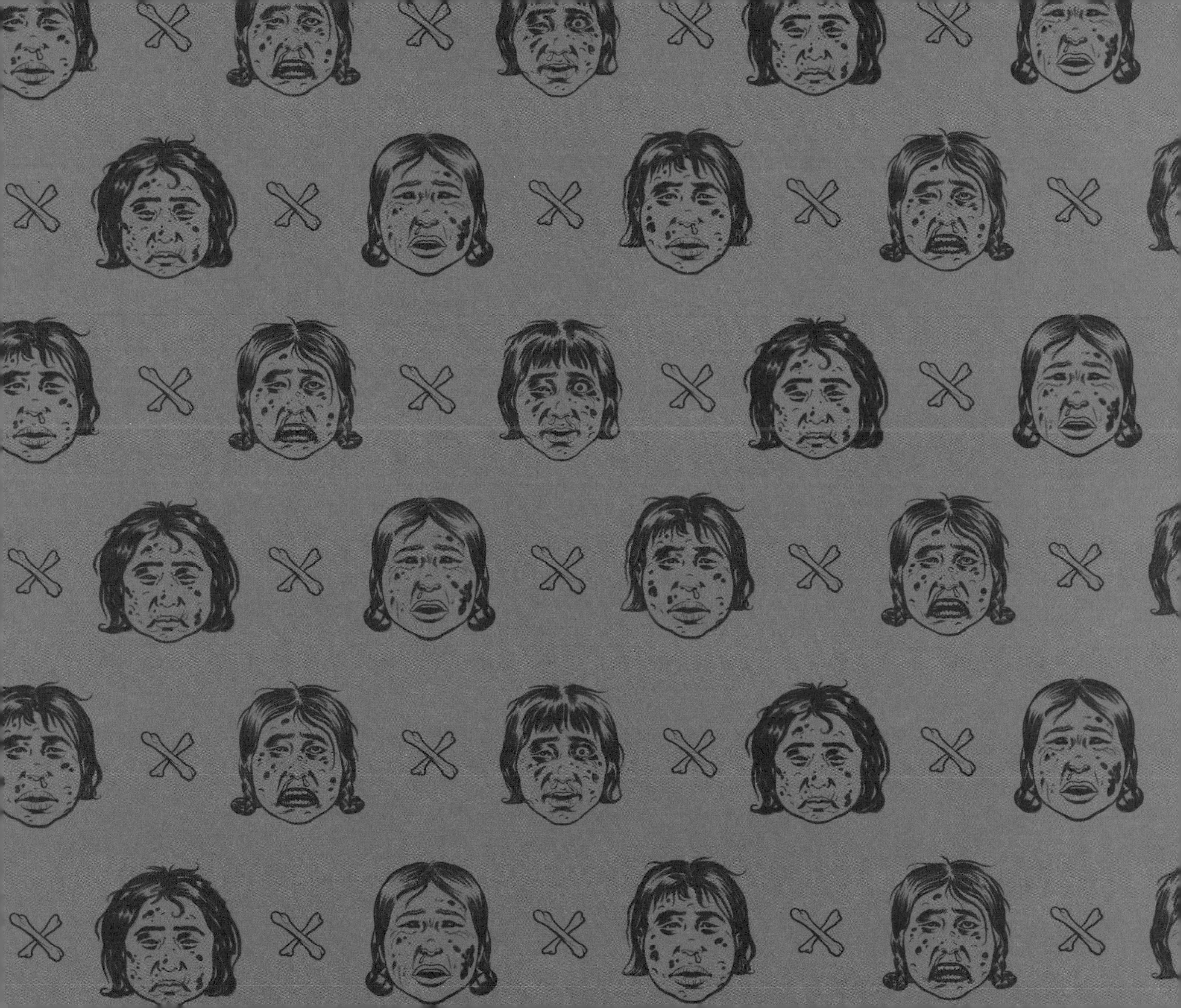

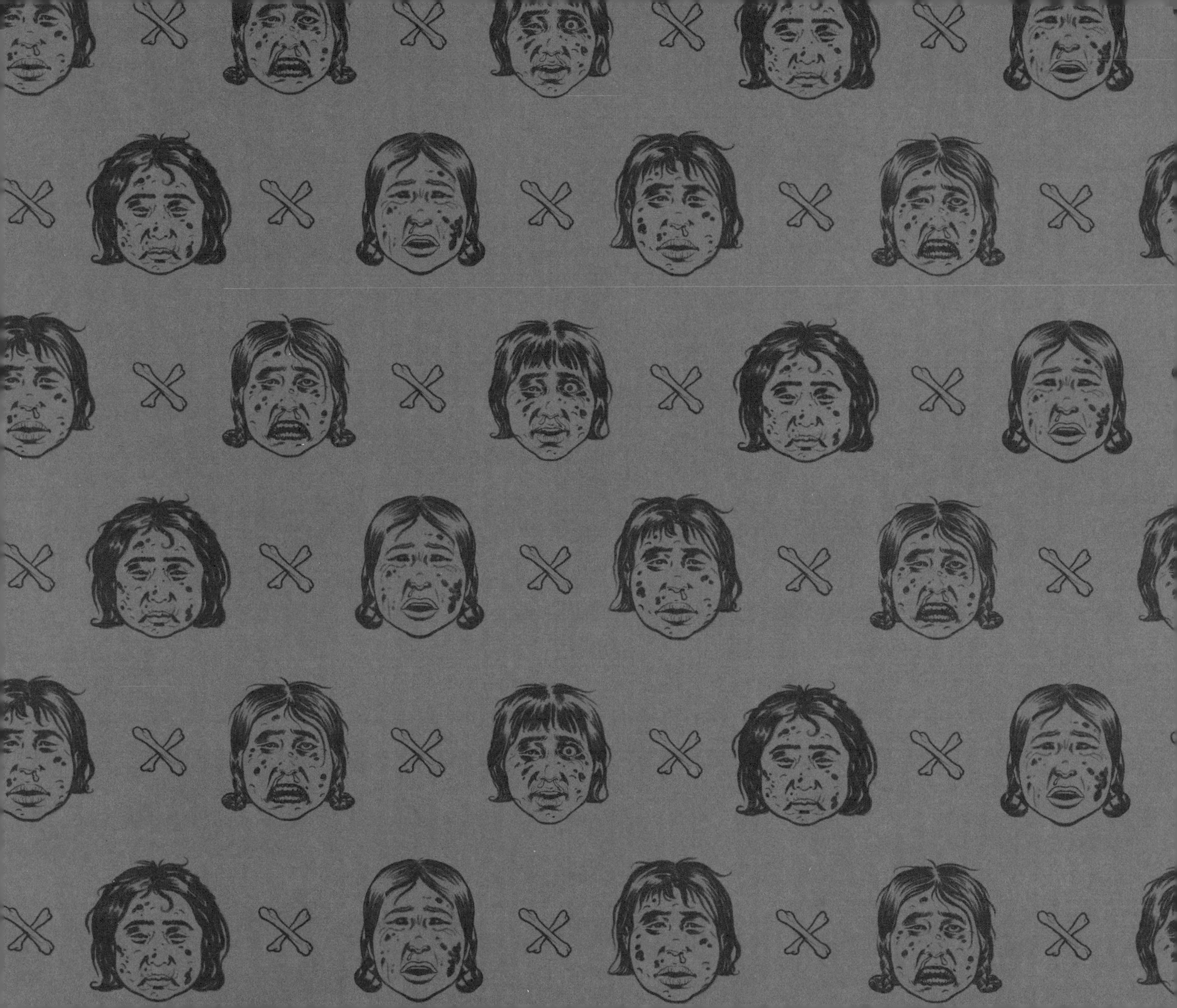